his perfect little heirs

his perfect little heirs

NICCI HARRIS

also by nicci harris

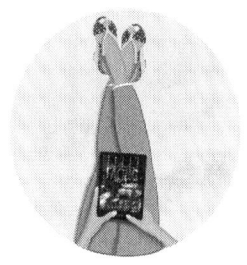

The Kids of The District

Facing Us

Our Thing

Cosa Nostra

Her Way

His Pretty Little Burden

His Pretty Little Queen

Their Broken Legend

Black Label Nicci Harris

<u>*CurVy 13*</u>

<u>*CurVy Forever*</u>

ISBN ebook: 978-1-922492-25-8

ISBN print: 978-1-922492-26-5

Edited by Mostert-Seed Editing

www.mostertseedediting.com

Internal graphics by Nicci Harris

Cover design by Ashes & Vellichor

his perfect little heirs

notes

This is an **epilogue novella** for The Kids of the District series—a Happily Ever After for our Butcher Boys.

It is not a standalone romance novella.

Not read their stories yet?

Start with Our Thing: Max and Cassidy's story. This series isn't a small bite, easy read. It is an emotive narrative that is deceptively complex.

Just in it for some spice?

Dive straight into this novella that has very little plot and a lot of love, family, and spice.

meet the couples

Get ready for spice in almost every chapter of this pregnancy novella featuring three Mafia brothers and their expecting partners.

Clay and Fawn:

Clay and Fawn are an unlikely couple.

Where she is wild and bohemian, he is controlled, regimented, and twice her age.

In this short, steamy read, Fawn tries to trust her body again after a previous loss. And Clay, the ruthless Don of the *Cosa Nostra*, learns how to compromise for his much younger fiancé.

Bronson and Shoshanna:

Shoshanna and Bronson are childhood sweethearts.

They have had difficulty conceiving, but their happiness knew no bounds when their son was born.

Fast forward a few years, and another baby is on the way, but this time Shoshanna struggles with the toll pregnancy number two takes on her body.

Max and Cassidy:

Max and Cassidy are complete opposites—he is grumpy; she is sunshine; he is tall and muscular; she is short and petite.

Max's stoicism is notorious, but the love he feels for his gentle wife is explosive.

He was absent for Cassidy's last pregnancy and the birth of his first child, so now that she is pregnant again, Max can finally fill that deep void.

*Author notes: This is an **epilogue** novella for The Kids of the District series—a Happily Ever After for our Butcher Boys. Not read their stories yet? Start with Our Thing: Max and Cassidy's story. This series isn't a small, bite-size, easy read. It is an emotive narrative that is deceptively complex. **Just in it for the spice?** Dive straight into this novella, featuring very little plot and a lot of love, family, and spice.*

CHAPTER ONE

fawn

My dear friend, Xander Butcher, told me that good things
come in threes:

Clay Butcher: Number one.

His heir: Number two.

Family: Number three.

And soon, I'll understand what the last two wonderful
things really mean.

On my knees at the feet of the deadliest man in the city,
the Don of the *Cosa Nostra*, Clay Butcher, I lay with my head
on his thigh while he reads the paper.

I steady my heart.

Hold my stomach.

I ignore the nerves racketing through me and focus on
Luna, stroking her fur and watching how she headbutts my
palm to get more affection. She meows and pads around, and
she's so fucking cute I want to smooch her face.

Will she sleep with the baby?

Is she allowed to?

The baby... The anticipation of meeting *number two* sits heavily inside my chest. I gaze up at Clay as his dark brows tighten, distinguished creases forming between them.

I nudge Clay's thigh a little, copying Luna.

Only he can settle the nerves.

What if the ultrasound is bad?

What if he's wrong... again?

What if he's small or twisted?

Is that a thing?

What if I break him?

What if he—

"I know you're nervous, sweet girl." Clay responds to my silent need, moving his hand to caress my hair, fingers gliding down the blonde strands to the ribbony tips.

Will I have time for him when we have children?

Oh God, will he have time for me?

I sigh. "Are *you* nervous, Sir?"

"Such a sweet question. Don't concern yourself with me today. Should we redirect your thoughts while you wait?"

My cheek rubs along his pants as I nod excitedly, and he places the paper beside him, widening his thighs.

He reaches for a pillow and places it on the floor, nodding an order to it. "Mount it. I want you humping the pillow gently while you suck on me. Do it now."

My coy eagerness plays across my cheeks, creating crimson hues. I will always blush for him. It is impossible not to.

Obediently, I climb onto the pillow. Seeking that blissful buzz, I rub along the fluffy mound as I reach up and draw his zipper down.

"Wait, sweet girl." He grips my wrists, then positions me, placing my palms flat on his knees. Straightening, I gaze up at him, and his dark intent flares through his blue eyes as they train on my mouth.

I part my lips to breathe beneath the intensity of his heated gaze, but then he orders, "More. Open your mouth wide for me. I want to see your tonsils."

My pulse flutters along my neck with nervous excitement as I widen my lips, my tongue wiggling around with uncertainty. I don't know where to put it. Saliva builds. I try to fight it. Not wanting to literally drool, although I figuratively do it often.

He grins. "Good girl. Stick your tongue out, and rest it on your lower lip. That's the most comfortable spot for you, and relax, sweet girl. You look pretty when you salivate for me."

My eyes well up when he pushes two fingers between my lips, fingering my mouth suggestively, his eyes unwavering from the action. He uses them to lather my mouth.

Stirring around my cheeks.

I mewl a little when a small stream of saliva slides from my bottom lip, but he only chuckles deeply. "Such a good girl. Now suck on my fingers and hump your pillow, little deer."

I stare up at him through my top lashes and envelop his fingers, gently sucking on them.

My wide gaze fixes on him, daring him. I suck harder and start to ride the pillow, feeling pleasure spinning around me, dizzying me. The moment is intimate. Exposing. I moan around his fingers, the desire between my thighs warming from the base of my spine to the tips of my ears.

His eyes darken when I shudder.

I close mine, unable to hold his.

I ride the pillow shamelessly. Suck his fingers. Curl my toes. Put on a show.

Moving and gyrating on my knees, I hum to the subtle pleasure between my thighs, the soft material lightly fondling my wet, pulsing core.

His fingers slip from inside my mouth, but I keep my eyes closed, my mouth parted, and my pussy grinding on the pillow for him to watch and enjoy.

I hear him shuffle.

My heart races.

The smooth, large head of his erection slides into my mouth, and I close my lips over it on a satisfied sigh. He is mine to enjoy. Only mine.

Softly, I suck, rewarded with a deep praise-filled groan.

Smoothing down my hair, he says, "You're going to meet the next love of your life soon, sweet girl, and you're going to do just fine. Everything will be perfect. The ultrasound will be fine. He will be strong. Resilient. Brave. How could he not be with a mother like my little deer," he says easily, but his voice is rough as his words of affirmation spur me on, my mouth licking him to match his praise. "*Christ*, little deer. Your mouth is so pretty. So eager." He lifts his hips and massages the back of my head, fingers circling my scalp, curling my hair around my crown. "Remember, little deer, that just because you have this very important responsibility, doesn't mean I am not here to guide you. Just because I have more to care for now, doesn't mean my priorities will change. Your wellbeing and safety will always be my number one focus. So, when you feel overwhelmed and you need reassurance, I am here. I will *always* put my little deer first. Will always choose you, so you can put my children first, so you can always choose them. Now, nod your head so I know you understand."

I nod around his cock.

"Good. You need to come on the pillow for me, sweet girl. Show me how pretty you are."

Yes, Sir.

Still mouthing his thick length, I focus on the pillow between my thighs, bunching it to a point. I ride it and whine around his cock, saliva rushing down my chin as the delicate sensation buzzes along my folds.

My rhythm breaks, becoming uneven as pressure builds through my core. Tightness gathers along my inner thighs. Heat races across my skin as a small orgasm slides through me. I release his cock. A gentle whimper whispers passed my lips, my body jerks softly on the pillow, and he praises me as I come.

"You are very endearing to watch, sweet girl. Such a good girl for me. Showing me how your pretty body moves, letting me smell your pretty scent." His voice is like velvet, and I shudder through my orgasm. "There you go. Do you feel a little bit better?"

I nod, my body a humming vessel of pleasure. A subtle kind of pleasure that is easy to feel and float down from. Nothing explosive like what he tears from me, but nice all the same when experienced under his gaze. "I feel good."

"You look very pretty." He reaches out and brushes his thumb down my cheek. "I like you blushing." I smile at him, and his soft expression balloons my heart. "Time to go, little deer. Up you get."

On wobbly legs, I rise in front of him. He tucks his cock back in his pants, standing with me. We fix ourselves for company and head towards the room I was taken to on my first morning staying here. When I heard my baby's heartbeat but didn't see— I didn't get to see him. It seems like such a long time ago. I was just a lost girl with no place in this world to call my own.

I know my place now—beside the most powerful man in the city. His rose. My thorns.

That thought settles all my nerves, and I enter the room with a new wave of enthusiasm.

Everything will be fine.

"Don't be nervous. Bronson and Luca have Kelly and

Stone, so it's just us," Shoshanna says as she sets up the machine while Cassidy slides onto the bed. Her eyes are soft and easy, whereas Max is filling the space as he always does, with his broad shoulders and guard-dog-like readiness that is always on.

His eyes are on his wife's face and not on her stomach or the machines, almost as though he doesn't want to look yet or... isn't ready to, maybe? I don't understand the reluctance in his gaze, but I know he was away for most of Cassidy's last pregnancy and missed the birth.

Does that affect him today?

Cassidy smiles at me from the high hospital-style bed as she pulls her shirt up and tucks the pink fabric in her bra. "Come up here with me, Fawn. We can both fit."

"Little one," Max protests, disapproval in his tone.

"Come on, Menace"—she reaches out her hand and squeezes his forearm— "There is plenty of room for us both. It's more fun." She lowers her voice, but I still hear her whisper to him, "It's still me and you. It's still *our thing.*"

Smiling, I crawl up beside her and we settle in, shoulder to shoulder, as Shoshanna applies the gel and presses the wand to Cassidy's belly. "Let's see this little Butcher."

I pull my shirt up and turn to Clay, who watches me with that smooth confidence he wears so easily.

I grin at him, and he strides to my bedside, casting a shadow on me that further settles my soul. Safety. His ominous, dark shadow is everything I dreamed of as a child growing up in the foster system.

Shoshanna draws me from him as she says, "There is your bub, Cassidy... Max?" She looks over at him, as the quiet in the room suddenly fills with the sound of a heartbeat. His baby's heart. "There's your baby's heartbeat."

"*Hi,*" Cassidy coos sweetly.

Lifting Cassidy's hand, Max holds it to his lips as though

it's his tether, her touch offering enough support for his gaze to finally meet the screen.

It's clearly a baby—a baby shape. I know why they call it the fetal position now.

Will mine look like that?

A few moments pass as Shoshanna measures the grey and black shapes that wobble around. And I think the look in Max's stare is enough to break the moon in half with its intensity.

Content, Shoshanna sighs. "The baby is perfect, Max."

Max can't talk.

"Oh, Max." Cassidy sits up and he leans down to take her into his arms, burying his face in her shoulder and hair. "I know, Menace. I know."

Shoshanna continues, "Are you coming back in a few weeks so I can tell you the sex?" She touches her own swelling stomach. "Bronson and I are going to wait. Have you thought about it?"

I know she didn't ask me, but I answer anyway, my own eagerness getting the better of my patience. "I wanna wait, too. Old school style. Under the moon. In a pool. A doula. Clay pacing beside me."

"Do I look like the kind of man who paces?"

I laugh because Sir is far too controlled to outwardly portray anxiety like that. "No."

Cassidy's soft voice says, "Max?"

He pulls back from her hold, hitting her with a stormy grey gaze bursting with truth. It's there. Hidden within firmly constructed walls is the most consuming love. "You choose, little one."

She uses her finger to smooth the ridge between his brows —his permanent scowl of perpetual concern. "We wait."

"Your turn, Fawn. This will be cold," she says as she applies the cool gel to my stomach. And now that the attention is on me, butterflies fill my body. I'm worried I might do something wrong, that something might already be wrong, that I've failed.

Would he forgive me if I lost another baby? *His* baby? I couldn't bear it.

Then, the wand touches me. I remember this part. The last time I was pregnant it all happened so fast. I felt removed, a bit like a monkey or a pet. I didn't feel as though the baby was mine, but today— I look over at Sir, and this time, he's not staring at the screen. He is looking at me.

While the wand touches my stomach, as it moves through the jelly, when it applies pressure to a specific spot, Clay Butcher looks at me. "Aren't you going to look at the screen, Sir?"

"After you do, little deer."

I didn't get to see him last time.

Thank you, Sir.

A tear rises to the corner of my eye, but I fight to keep it still, and look at the display just as the same shape appears. A baby shape.

Wait... What is that?

A little bit of air hitches as I inhale sharply at the lovely sight. Then... A heartbeat. *No...* That sounds different, looks different, *God. Is everything okay?*

Is he broken?

Did I break him already?

Did I break him again!

I cover my mouth as tears fall down my face, panic reaching up and grabbing me so fast I barely have time to breathe. I don't feel Clay's hand take mine until his thumb moves over my fingers.

It grounds me.

"*Fawn,*" Shoshanna says my name with amazement

wrapped around each letter. "You're having twins. There are two beautifully formed fetuses here."

What?

"*Christ.*" I hear Sir mutter from beside me, and I glance at him quickly, then back at the monitor. "You're perfect, sweet girl. Look what you're making for me."

Shoshanna starts to measure the screen and type into the keyboard. While it all happens, I clear my throat a few times, but don't try to talk because my voice will wobble and crack if I do. I'm overwhelmed.

Twins.

Two.

But—But good things come in three...

Clay Butcher: Number one.

His heir: Number two.

Family: Number three.

This is four... *Two* heirs. This means I need to start from one again... because— No.

A smile hits my cheeks as the two embryos bounce around each other on the screen. And I decide right now, I can just keep counting to... to *forever.*

Good things don't come in three.

Good things have no limit.

Baby number two: Number four.

CHAPTER TWO

fawn

I shouldn't be nervous as I press on the brake with my Converse. My tawny leather skirt sits mid-thigh, and my long-sleeved white body suit clings to my figure, showing off the bump at my lower stomach where butterflies zoom around and babies grow in the figurative flapping of their wings.

I don't need to be nervous.

After several lessons with Clay, I can easily drive around Connolly's streets.

For a man who lives by his own rules, a man of infallible nature, he sure likes it when *I* obey the law.

1: Flat shoes to drive.

2: Two hands on the wheel at all times.

3: Look in the mirrors every five seconds.

Yes, Sir.

There are no other cars on the road. He won't let me drive during peak hours or even on a main road. I am not allowed to go over forty kilometres an hour. The only reason he is allowing me to do this at all is because he promised to give me anything I wish. I want to learn to drive.

Beside me, Clay pretends his blue gaze isn't panoramic and measured. He pretends that relinquishing control doesn't unnerve him. If I didn't know him so well, the smooth way he sits and his relaxed expression, would sell the idea.

He hates this.

I smile at the shiny red bonnet. "What type of car is this? Is it fast? Is it a hybrid? We should consider the environment because we have enough money to be mindful, don't you think?"

"Attention on the road."

"I'm a woman; I can do two things at once."

"Excellent. You are driving and growing my children inside you. Such a clever girl. Now, attention on the road."

"You're so condescending, Sir."

"I will indulge this conversation another time. Your safety is more important to me than your sensitivities are," he declares. I slowly sigh, so he adds, "Christ, fine, it's a BMW."

Grinning, I focus on the road.

Ahead, I need to take a left, so I indicate, but a grey car is idling on the side of the road, and as I turn the corner, I edge too wide, narrowly missing the taillight.

The man looks up from his GPS and honks the horn before yelling, "Fucking look where you're going!"

The commotion shocks my pulse to race into my ears.

"I'm sorry," I say to the car even though it can't hear me because it's an inanimate object and the man can't hear me because he's inside it, and— I'm losing my mind. "I'm so sorry. Fuck. I *am* a shit driver. I'm so sorry. I can't do two things at once; I can't even do one. I'm failing."

Somewhere muted in the sea of pregnancy hormones, rational thought flickers—I know I'm being erratic.

Everything just erupts these days. A week back, Jasmine and I were allowed to get a coffee together in the city with only a few guards—in sight. I'm sure there were more.

That day, I saw a seat by the window and mentally sat there. After I had ordered my tea, Jasmine and I found it already taken… and I cried. I. *Cried.* Like, full-blown, how could this happen, that was meant to be for me, this isn't fair —*cried.*

And now, my shaky hands fist the wheel and tears spill down my cheeks. My heart races, and the energy beside me is now neither smooth nor relaxed. It's electrified.

I try not to look at Clay.

Because I can't fucking do two things at once.

Then, in the rear-view mirror, I watch as one of our black cars parks behind the grey one, another in front, and one parallel to it. The three vehicles lock the car in.

I blanch. "What's happening? It was my fault."

"Take this roundabout and head back towards the car, sweet girl," Clay says, his voice taking on the chilling tone of apathy that I have come to know as a dangerous sound.

I do as he instructs, and then pull over just ahead of the convoy of cars.

Once the BMW is in park, I stare ahead, nerves still rattling through me, adrenaline a little potent in my veins.

Clay places his finger under my chin and directs me to him, asking, "Did that scare you?"

I blink at the most powerful man in the city… *Hell,* maybe the world. "It was my fault, Sir. I went too wide. I fucked up, and I *disappointed* you."

"No, you did not disappoint me. But you did miscalculate the turn." He nods, his clear blue gaze melting into me. "You were too pleased with yourself for winning our conversation. You need more practise, little deer. You can learn to drive, but there is no need for it. You will not be driving yourself around."

"I know that."

"Good." He leans in and kisses me, dissolving my nerves for a moment under his sweet attention.

Too soon, his lips leave mine and he steps from the vehicle. Smoothing his dark tie down his black shirt, he turns and walks to the grey vehicle that idles quietly.

With wide eyes, I twist to watch my fiancé approach the car that honked at me, and the man being dragged from it by my first guard, Bolton. Or, as I affectionately call him: Henchman Jeeves.

The man who barked at me looks to be in his late twenties, with blond hair and of average build, wearing jeans and a blue shirt with a wave print on it. Contradictory to his casual attire, the lush fabric of Clay's black suit moves with each long, meaningful stride as he stalks towards him.

Stopping in front of the vehicle, Clay clasps his hands and waits as Henchman Jeeves presents the man like a gift or offering for him.

Unsettled, I twist the ends of my hair around my finger, but the houses lining the street remind me that nothing too dire can happen. Not here. In this quiet neighbourhood.

But... It was my fault.

The man is still. I can only see the back of Sir's head now, but the man is nodding nervously. He wipes at his forehead, even though the cool breeze holds the climate at the perfect temperature.

Suddenly, the man looks at me.

Clay clicks to draw his attention.

The man with the blue shirt snaps his eyes back in place and continues to shrink a few feet through the intense conversation. He was already pocket-sized compared to Clay Butcher, but most people are.

Several moments pass, and it's near silent on this street. Not a single car. It is as though Clay blocks part of the city whenever I have a lesson.

Oh. My. God.

He blocks the streets.

When Clay and the man wander toward my car, I exhale fast. Quickly, I slouch back in the seat as though I wasn't watching the exchange.

Chill, Fawn.

The man knocks on the driver's side windscreen with Clay standing just behind him, an ominous presence at his spine.

I lower the window, and Clay kicks the man's shoe to encourage him to step backwards, to add space.

"Miss, I am so sorry for yelling at you." The man stammers. "I- I—"

I interrupt, "I went—"

"No. You have a—"

"Do *not*"—Clay's voice booms—"interrupt her."

The man swallows. "My apologies."

"I overshot the turn," I finish softly.

"You have a Learner sign on your car, Miss. I shouldn't have been on the side of the road. I should have been—"

"*Considerate,*" Clay grounds.

The man agrees with a nod. "Yes."

"Now, be a good boy and tell her that you didn't have your hazard lights on; therefore, it was your fault."

"Yes," he says, sweat gathering across his brows. "I didn't have my hazards on. You probably couldn't see me properly."

This is surreal, but my panic has mellowed some. Pregnancy does that, too. A whirlwind. One minute you're crying and the next, laughing. And I wipe the tears from my eyes, feeling better about this conversation. "That's okay. We all forget things sometimes."

"No. It is not *okay*." Clay lifts his chin to the distance, dismissing the man—*the Clay Butcher nod*. "Leave. *Now*."

The man jogs quickly to his car, his shoulders dropping with relief as he is allowed to climb back into his vehicle, unharmed but clearly rattled.

I arch an eyebrow at Sir. "That wasn't fair."

Something carnal with warning moves through his clear blue gaze. "Did your eyebrow just give me attitude, little deer?"

I relax my forehead. "*Um..*"

He drinks me in through slow lusty strokes, before adjusting his tie at his thick neck. "You heard the boy,"—he opens the car door and gestures with a nod for me to step from the driver's side—"He didn't have his hazards on."

"He's not really a *boy*—"

"To me, he is." Clay darts his unamused gaze between me and the open car door he is silently signalling me through.

"Okay." I crawl across the centre console and nestle into the seat, crossing my legs, unable to stifle my glee when he growls with frustration at still holding the door open.

"Are you being facetious on purpose, sweet girl?"

I bite my lip to hide my budding smile. "I don't know what facetious means, Sir."

He ducks into the driver's seat and with a roar of the engine—a noise I didn't know this car could make. "Purposely difficult. Treating serious situations with mockery." He pulls out onto the quiet suburban street.

"Oh." I smile harder. "Then yes. I am."

We pull into a drop-off circle under the shelter of a grand canopy, where a man rushes to open Clay's car door and take his keys. I sit and wait like a good girl.

Clay circles the car and opens my door. This time, I step from the vehicle, and he places his hand on my lower back to guide me into the store.

Immediately, I'm confused as we enter the large rectangular room that ends with an impressive, exposed-brick fireplace. It takes me a few moments to deduce we are *not* in a restaurant because although there are tall, cushioned stools in dark leather and women and men drinking champagne at high marble counters, in front of them are glass display cases.

Each couple has an attendant, a pretty woman or handsome man showing them various pieces of jewellery.

Oh. My. God.

It's a jewellery store.

Keep your cool, Fawn.

I stop midstride. "A jewellery store?" I touch the diamond-encrusted butterfly pendant around my neck, the strategically set spotlights overhead dancing inside the facets. "I have this. I don't need an—" Then it hits me, but I'm too dazed to speak. I find myself walking with his assistance to a private room behind the fireplace.

It is a miniature replica of the larger room but with one case and two chairs. I approach the display. Inside the navy moulds are rings. Only four. Each with a different band, clasp, and setting. Two are solitaire. Two have smaller diamonds haloing the larger one. The central rock is the same size in each and the same shape. My pulse thrums along my neck.

Stunned, I stare at the rings when a hand slides across my jaw to direct my eyes to our female attendant as she opens a small square box with a large blue round-shaped diamond inside.

My breath hitches.

The lady says, "This is the one, Mr Butcher."

I knew this was coming. He proposed to me weeks ago. I

was lying across his lap on the sofa in our room, and he was playing with my body. The aroma of coffee and the flick of newspaper sheets, have come to arouse me. It can be quite inconvenient at times.

This early morning, he had insisted I read to him while he touched me. But the papers he gave me to read were divorce papers signed with a kiss—a blessing—from Aurora. He then stood me in front of him, so his lips brushed my swelling stomach, and said against the flesh,

"Although I will kneel for you, sweet girl, and the children you make for me, should you ask me, I will endeavour to put you all on a pedestal, so I need not to."

Drawn back to the elegant room, bathed in a warm hue, I watch in awed silence as Clay picks up the diamond and scrutinises the rock with obvious familiarity. The attendant is smiling at him, pinkened by the stunning diamond or the magnificent man holding it; I don't know which.

Clay hums and then says, "Lovely." It's not unlike the decadent sound he makes when spreading my legs.

I press my thighs together as that deep, impressed rumble spindles through me. He told me once he would train me to be needy for him, to be ready, his, and I am. I really am. I clear my throat, but my voice is shaky as I say, "It's blue."

"Yes."

"Aren't diamonds usually white?"

"Boron." He smiles smoothly at me before sweeping his eyes down to where my feet move against my efforts to stop my body from rocking towards his. I want that sound again. "I presume you don't know much about diamonds, sweet girl. Most of the women I know would be fainting in the presence of this diamond."

"Are you disappointed that I'm not fainting?"

He juts his chin towards the door, and the attendant leaves. When he leans in close, his lips hovering by my ear.

"No," he purrs. "I'm very pleased my little deer is wet, instead. Was it the sound I made? Or the latte aromatics burning in the corner?" I flush *everywhere*. I twist to see a candle burning, and yes, it's coffee scented. Heat brims in places that throb for him.

He straightens and says, "Both, I imagine. Let me tell you about her before I spread you open on this cabinet and taste between your thighs." I swallow, and he sets the diamond in my palm where I move her—*it*—around with my finger. "She is quite the enigma," he goes on. "Most diamonds of this calibre have a long, precise history, but the reports of her are unclear. She was owned by royalty and then disappeared. We know she was dug up in the seventeenth century, and experts say she was cut from the same stone as the Hope Diamond."

I look up at him. "The one from *Titanic*?"

His chuckle is deep and delicious and not helping the wetness gathering against the fabric of my underwear. "The one that *inspired* the one from *Titanic*, yes. She is the same colour as your right eye, little deer, and if you like her, all you need to do is pick your band and clasp, and they will have her made for you."

"For me..." The words trail to a shocked sigh. "How do I thank you, Sir? For everything you have done for me? For this"—I widen my arms— "life."

"You don't thank me, little deer. Not for this. It would be an insult. This is not a favour or a gift. It is your right. It is my great privilege to touch you, to take you, taste you, have your trust in all things, your body beneath mine, your watery eyes looking up at me when you suck my cock. It is my *greatest* privilege to spoil you as you do me."

Plucking the diamond from my palm, he places it back in the box and slides it to the side.

I hold my breath as he retrieves the four rings from inside the display and places them in my hand. Exhaling, I accept them. Before I can study each clasp or band, he lifts me to sit on the display case, my skirt hiking up further, flashing him with white lace knickers. "Play with your pretty things while I play with mine."

He twists me to lay flat along the glass case until *I* am the damn display. I stare at the four rings as he spreads my legs on the counter and moves to the end.

He loosens the tie around his neck, his own greedy need for me revealed in that action. "You're blushing across your thigh skin," he groans, dipping down to trail his tongue from my knee to my wet centre. "So pretty."

Moans cascade from me as he laps up the wetness trailing down my inner thigh. His nose is in my knickers now, inhaling. I sigh with relief at the heat of his breath. This man *is* my orgasm, has made me his in every way. Tuned my body like an instrument to his specific way of play.

I fight the roll of my eyes as he eats me through my knickers. Focused on the gold band, it instantly stands out to me, but then the rose-coloured one is also prett— *God.*

He slides the fabric away.

I hitch my legs over his shoulders, cuddling his head and neck into me. "I can't pick," I breathe, then whimper as his hot tongue circles my clit. "I can't—" I buck when he sucks the bud in, and *God...* the skill this man has. It shouldn't be legal. "I can't concentrate."

"I know the one you will choose, little deer."

"How can you? When I have no idea."

"*Christ*, the taste of you is painful at times." He slides two fingers into me and starts to fuck, encouraging more slickness into his mouth.

Stars scatter behind my eyes.

Fuck.

This.

Is.

Too.

Good.

The sound of his fingers fucking me and his lips lapping greedily fills the room with thick arousal. A very real energy. Lusty. Dark. Tangible force.

I pant under the attention. Bucking as my chest grows tighter, the weight of need sitting heavy on me.

It's perfect.

Right there.

That... place.

I cry out as pleasure floods me with sweet— He stops. He damn cuts the orgasm off mid-detonation, dropping the pressure, making me dizzy and frantic for my release.

"Sir," I beg and roll in his palms. *"Please."*

I hear the dark amusement in his voice as he growls, "Discipline for that *facetious* eyebrow and for crawling across the centre console like a child."

I bow to his lips. *"Sir."*

"Easy, sweet girl. I will never leave you needy. When you pick your ring, I will let you come." He slides his tongue the length of my wet folds, the gradual and steady stimulation intent on grounding his devious demand. "Choose. You deserve these. You are being cautious instead of accepting that you may have whichever pleases you. What pleases me is sitting softly in my hands and dripping down my tongue. I do not want you to be prideful today. Not over this. Pick."

His finger touches my puckering hole and I gasp, instantly pressing back on him, greedy to feel the exquisitely odd stretch, so uncomfortable, so obscene. And dark. And I love it. His finger *there* is my favourite. I want it, I want it—I'm desperate for it. "Please, Sir." I writhe around on the cabinet, greedy for the sensation.

"Choose."

God.

I lift each ring to my face as he licks me softly—not enough, not nearly enough. The gold. The white. The rose-coloured one... I lift my hips to grind on his face.

"My little pussy," he says, awed and gruff, in love with what he is gazing at. "Always wanting to be pet and played with. I like her open. Like her supple for me." He circles my special hole again, and the sound that leaves me bites and rumbles. "Sir! Please."

"Choose, little deer."

I growl.

The white.

With the delicate clasp.

White and blue.

Like the moon in the sky.

Like the stars reflected in the ocean.

White and blue.

"The white one," I decide, and as I do, he presses the tip of his finger through the tight muscles, sucks my clit into his mouth, and rockets me over the edge of sanity, forcing a ripple of sensation to every inch of my body. I gyrate my pelvis upward while a cry tears from my mouth.

I come hard.

CHAPTER THREE

cassidy

5TH MONTH

Another early morning like the last, Max isn't in bed with me, and I know why.

Oh, Menace.

I adore all the little contradictory pieces of my Max, but the stubborn ones are often hard to endure. Those ones keep him from me. Keep him from himself, too.

I wrap my arms around my middle, cuddling the fluffy pink robe to my body. Maybe it's the hormones rushing me or the ensuing throbbing between my legs, but I am walking across the dewy grass under the ambient early morning sun to find him.

I reach the outhouse—his gym and my ballet studio. Pushing the door open, warmth floods me instantly. Max Butcher offers far more radiant heat to my soul than any fluffy robe can.

I stay like a little voyeur, watching my six-foot-four lover as he works out. He grips the high beam, pulling his long, large body up to his chin. Controlled and powerful, he repeats chin up after chin up, the cords and muscles in his arms pulsing, rolling. He's an athlete. Like me.

"Menace," I whisper his name, but he sees me in the studio mirror at the same time. He drops to his feet and turns to face me. Sweat slides down his face, the beads rolling over a tight jaw that was probably pulsing through his musings.

"Little one." He sounds unimpressed. I smile at that. "Go back to bed."

Despite his order, he strides towards me, and I imagine him lifting me to straddle him, feeding his hand under my bum and stroking my entrance as we kiss before laying me down beneath him and taking what he needs from me.

But he doesn't do that.

He tugs the robe tighter and runs his big hands down my arms to create warmth with the friction. *But I am already warm, Menace.*

I crane my neck to gaze into his storm-grey eyes. "I want this to stop."

His brows pinch. "What?"

"The early morning workouts." I blush. "I miss *our* early morning workout."

"Little one," he sighs roughly, his hand sliding down my body, hitching my breath in anticipation, only to stop on the lower curve of my abdomen where our second child grows willingly and strong—like him. "I'm too big. I'll lick you all better." He smirks, the curve provocative but hiding his true concerns. The ones about the baby. And me.

All the time.

Every sneeze.

Cough.

I kicked my toe on the door the other day. It bled and I cried. So, I found him fastening foam edging across the skirting boards the following evening. "It's not like that, Max. My cervix is protecting him. Come on. You know this."

He goes on, "I'll lick you all day if you need me to."

"Listen to me—"

"I'm too big for even you, Cassidy."

"I like the feel. I like—"

"*Dammit.* I feel like I'm tearing you open sometimes."

"Stop." I touch his rough jaw.

I want *him.* I push his hand under my robe and cup between my thighs so he can feel the heat and need as I rock in the warm hold. I moan as I say, "I need more. I want you. On top of me. Thrusting. Vulnerable. *Max*—" I breathe his name through deep-seated arousal, and he locks his jaw around his own groan as these thoughts play across my face. "*Please.*" Shamelessly, I rub on him, needing the grunts, the deep massage of his erection… "I need you inside me. I need to feel you."

His eyes darken to blue rings of lust and torment. While I feel myself leaking through my knickers and on to his hand, feeling loose, he stares at me.

Then, he catches me, threading his other arm around my middle, holding me to him. And I think I've won. He slides his fingers under the wet fabric, pushing two inside me with a possessive groan.

His voice is deep when he says, "Wet little one."

I buck to the sensation of being full of those long, thick, skilled fingers. My legs give out, but he's holding me now. He knew I'd go weak at his touch. He knows *me.*

With his fingers moving slowly inside me, he lowers me to the studio floor. A deep voice floats past my ears, the dark tempo curling my toes. "To this day, I feel like my touch taints you." Using the mass of his arm to hold me off the hard surface, his large hand cradles the back of my head; he eases in and out of me as we meet the floor. "I'll always feel this way, little one. You're too sweet for me."

I like this Max.

The one that consumes me.

My eyes roll under his intense gaze.

Soft sounds of pleasure escape me as I roll my pelvis, lifting, chasing a deeper penetration. The fit is already tight, but he's holding back. I'm swollen down there from the pregnancy. Still, I want more. "More, Max. I want to feel you."

He dips to lick my lips, and I open to suck his tongue into my mouth. Our kiss quickly becomes devouring. His hips start to rock against my thigh. And this is it... I get *him.*

Familiar tingles rush from my toes to my ears, a sensation that climbs, forcing my body to shudder all over in his consuming embrace. He works my core with precision, twisting his two fingers against my clinging walls.

I turn into a mewling mess.

Then, the sensation drowns my mind, confuses, distracting me from what I wanted... What I wanted... *God,* I whimper as his lips drag down my chin to my neck. My robe falls open. He tongues the divot at my collarbone, then trails wetly down.

Down.

Down.

No. Well, okay. Just a little lick.

My hands fly to grip his dark hair as he gently lays me on my back, so his large shoulders can settle between my thighs. Thick fingers stretch me. Push in. Through. Out.

God.

My mind swims in pleasure.

I close my eyes when his tongue moves between my folds, lapping upwards to my clit and down to where he fingers me. "Fuck. This pussy. All tainted by me. And all mine."

His rough words contract my muscles, jolting my back to

arch as my climax pools like a ball of heat at the point of his fingers and tongue. It's so good, but I want… I'm not going to come. I want him inside me. A shared orgasm.

Breathe, Cassidy.

A brimming mass of sensation taunts me. I tighten to stop from giving in completely. I can't come until he's inside me. I'm strong. In control.

Then the bristles on his jaw start to rub my soft thighs in the way that I like… and his tongue, *God*. His tongue threatens to end the pressure with every swipe, his sexy deep groans promise to enjoy it as much as I do, and his fingers guarantee my muscles fatigue in the most wonderful way.

Frick, I can't…

"Max." My head rolls. "I want…"

You!

I come hard, my toes curling on a cry when my orgasm explodes. The wave of energy now twitches through me as I fist his hair, close my thighs, and ride his face until the intensity drops to a hum. Frustration and relief both find me through my pleased, sated state. Damn butthead. He won. He tricked me.

Max lifts me into his arms, and I circle his neck with mine. My nose meets his cheek as he walks me outside and back to the main house.

I puff, grumpily. "You don't play fair."

Of course, he doesn't respond to my pouting. Even though it's true, I undoubtedly feel better. Relaxed. All the pregnancy hormones have been figuratively licked from me.

We pass Kelly's room.

I catch the way Max quickly checks our bodyguard, Carter, is outside our daughter's door. Back in our master suite, with the open-plan bathroom that displays a raised hot tub, he lays me down on the mattress like a feature.

Before he can leave, I grip the back of his neck, feeding my nails through his hair at the nape, holding him to me. The scent of my orgasm and Max Butcher—poisonous and sweet —suffuses me as I allow my body to loosen.

"Stay with us."

He stills. "I'm sorry, little one. I'm so fucking sorry; I'm a selfish bastard. I don't know how to do this. I don't—" He growls at himself. "I missed out last time, and this time…"

"I know." I swallow down the memories of carrying our daughter alone, of his absence during the labour, his absence those first few years. And for someone like Max Butcher, who can only show his love with physical acts and service, he literally couldn't love either of us for all that time…

"I love you, Max. You're a wonderful father. You don't need to do anything. I'll do it. Just trust me, Menace."

He tightens over me, and I soothe those parts of him that will never believe it by tickling his neck and up into his hair. I don't expect to hear "I love you" in return.

I don't want to.

Before Max went away, he promised me that when we start our life together, he would never say he 'loves me' because he would show me every day with his actions instead. It was a promise to never leave again. To be present. To be accountable. That's the kind of promise a girl dreams about. It's how Max lives. His actions need to have meaning. Words are so fickle. I accept him like this. The words… are just sounds, but his actions are ballads that melt and last, and it's how we love truthfully.

I close my eyes, and time stretches with us like this—his heart beats above mine, and his breath fans down my face. The memory of his tongue hums through my body and warms me. My Max. My Menace.

After several long moments, I feel him move down the bed and lay on his side, careful to not put weight on me. He reaches out and covers our baby with his warm palm.

The hold is gentle and possessive.

Pinpricks hit the backs of my eyes.

He begins to speak, an emotional and deep utterance that catches my breath and my soul along with it. "I don't know how to care for you when you're in there." Tears spill from the corners of my eyes, leaking down my temples. I wonder if he thinks I'm asleep. So, I keep them shut, stay still, and leave him with his unborn child.

"I can't show you how I feel about you. Or how much you mean to this family. To your sister. My wife. Me. I'll show you one day. If you can wait. Be strong. Be gentle with my wife. I can't live without her. And when you get out and take your first breath, I'll be there to hold you—first. I'll be there to show you with my actions the moment you are born how I feel about you, and every fucking day after that. I swear it."

He circles the small bump with his finger.

And I spill quiet, happy tears.

CHAPTER FOUR

bronson

I'm playing with my boy.

While the girls agreed to all wait until they're born to discover the sex, I just know. This is my boy re-embodied. A little bit of her, a little bit of me. It's him. The one that was ripped from us when we were teenagers.

My boy.

And I'll hold him soon.

Resting on my elbows, I use my miniature finger-BMX and do skids down Shoshanna's badarse stretch marks. Using the tiger stripes on her skin as a dirt track.

I make a screeching sound as the bike comes to a sudden diagonal stop at the boundary of her pubic line.

"Hazard ahead," I quietly call out, and Shoshanna rouses from her slumber. "Looks slippery."

Maybe I should go a little lower.

Test the depth...

Don't do it, Bronson.

I smirk. Rolling the bike lower until I get to her lovely folds, the image of my bike getting wedged between them, spinning the tyre over her clit to get out of—

"Don't you dare," she murmurs huskily.

"Good morning, baby," I say, sliding up from where I was playing with my boy to look his mum in the face.

Her near-black hair lies across her lips and chin, a perfect addition to her olive skin. Like, mine. We're both tanned. Me: half-Sicilian. Her: half-Egyptian. Our boy will probably be tanned, too.

"You look beautiful." She cocks an eye open, a brilliant amber orb glowing in the gathering sunlight. Exhausted, she scrunches her face up.

Stunning.

My beautiful distraction.

Every damn morning.

Every damn night.

My baby having my baby.

As I watch her, imagining our baby growing inside her, my cock expands along my leg. No one gets me harder than Shoshanna. Just the sight of her makes me ache.

"I'm so tired." She sighs heavily. "*God,* this pregnancy. It's zapping everything from me. I can't even think."

I think you're wondrous, baby.

Thank you for doing all the hard work.

"Sleep then." I trail the curve of her full tits with my hand, resisting the urge to bounce them around, and, instead, I head south. "I'll fuck you so gently, you'll—"

"No." She shoves me away from her and slides to the edge of the bed, pulling the sheet with her as she goes.

I frown, straightening on the mattress. "Where are you going? You said you were tired. Get your arse back here—"

"My *fat* arse."

Anger simmers inside me when she covers her luscious body with the sheet.

She calls over her shoulder. "I'm fat, and you're using me like a damn mountain range."

Don't say that, baby.

"I love mountains." I try to keep my voice even, but her insecurities never sit calmly inside my mind. "Hills. Ranges. You remember our lookout, baby?" The place we went to love each other when we were teenagers. There is nowhere I'd rather be than on a dirt track with my boys and my girl."

Sadness sits on her lips. "Sure."

Fuck this.

I jump to my feet and follow her into the bathroom. She is agitated as all hell, so I give her as much space as my cravings will allow. Grabbing my toothbrush, I get started on cleaning my pearly whites.

She stares at her reflection with disdain, and I hate it. Heat builds inside me. I want to warn her to stop looking at the girl I love like that.

I don't like it, baby.

Then she scowls at me towering behind her, and I feign innocence, "What? I'm just polishing."

I know she wants to be alone so she can scrutinise her magnificent body and internally hate on herself.

I'm not letting you do that.

She softens when my mouth fills with foam from the toothpaste and drips down my jaw. "You're such a nutcase." A sad smile moves across her lips. Rolling her eyes down my naked body, she lands on my cock which stands to attention for her. *Sir, yes, sir. At your command, baby.* "And you're so perfect." With a growl, she looks back at herself. "And I'm huge," she bites, but I just grin 'cause I love every inch. "Don't smile. Cassidy and Fawn still look lean, like they swallowed a small bowling ball, whereas I look like I've been gorging on cake for the past decade."

"I like cake."

"I'm a fucking whale." Dropping the sheet, she reveals her entire curved figure in the mirror. As though I don't know what she looks like, as though I don't stare at her when she sleeps and jerk off to the full mound of her tits. I dream about the way she bounces. She has never been hotter to me than she is now, carrying my boy.

Several stripes cut wicked lines over her swollen stomach, with more surely to join them. I rub oil on her skin every damn night, but she's prone to them or some shit. We're not spring chickens, either.

It's an age thing, maybe.

"Firstly." I come up behind her until my erection is pressed to her bare succulent arse. "Whales are majestic as fuck." Gritting the brush between my teeth, I talk around the spines and falling white foam. "Don't talk shit about whales, baby. Secondly" —I roll my cock in the thick seam of her arse cheeks— "I want more of you. More mountains. More tracks. More life." I grip the vanity on either side of her, flexing my fingers for her to see. "I got big hands, baby. Fill them up for me."

A reluctant smile tugs at the corner of her mouth. "Just brush your teeth, Nutcase. Stone will be awake soon."

Mischievous thoughts circle my mind. I lean over her, spit in the sink, and rinse the brush off. Then, I circle it around her stomach and dip it between her thighs. She presses them together. "Stop."

"It's a new brush, baby. It's clean."

"I'm not."

I force my knee between her thighs from behind, a little more aggressive than usual but I'm excited. *What can I say?* I wanna polish her plump bead. "Perfect."

With one hand on the vanity by her hip and one circling her and between her legs, I lock her in place. I slide the toothbrush between her folds. Wanting access, I press more of my leg between her thick thighs to widen them and spread her. Her pussy opens for me, so I use the soft bristles to stroke a circular path around her clit.

A tight moan leaves her lips, a spasm forcing her to plant both hands on the vanity top for stability. Just as though the soft spines have a direct link to her nerves. And now she is loving it. Her long, elegant fingers move like a wave on the granite in time with my brush.

Using the mirror to see perfectly, I circle the fat bead with the silky spines. It's like God knew I needed sensitive gums just so I could have this moment. I laugh to myself. "This reminds me of that day with the gun. You remember that, baby? How much you like to ride my Glock as much as you like to ride my cock. My lioness."

She closes her eyes through a shudder.

Then I warn her. "Don't look at my girl like that again," I breathe into her ear, dark severity a strain in my tone. "Don't look at my girl's body like that again. You owe this body Stone. You owe this body breath. Life. It is what I love. What I fuck. What I dream about. It is what I hold. Smell. Don't disrespect my girl's body in front of me again." My cock gets harder when she rocks on the bristles. Chasing. She wants more.

My balls grow heavy. I wedge my erection between her arse cheeks and rub myself in the channel while concentrating on the pregnant goddess panting and giving in to me.

Shoshanna's head drops back to the hard surface of my chest. Her eyelids dance as her eyes roll, and her lips part as she moans. I dip the brush down the quivering inner folds of her pussy and quickly back up to bear down on her clit again.

Enchanted, enraptured, even, I watch my beautiful distraction come apart at my skilled *motherfucking* hands. I lick my lips, the sight of her working me into a state of fever.

My vision closes in.

You're so hot, baby.

The threat of an orgasm wrenches a growl from me as I work my cock in the seam of her arse. If I wasn't infatuated with finishing her on my toothbrush, I'd lube myself up and fuck her arse at the same time.

"*Bronson,*" is all she can manage as I speed up, working her bud in insistent circles. "*Jesus Christ.* That's- that's- *Fuck!*"

The last word falls from her through a husky cry. The sound of her coming, the bouncing of her arse as she shudders in front of me, forces my balls to contract. Heat wraps around the base of my spine, and a groan rumbles from my chest as I shoot cum across her lower back and my abdomen.

I try not to fall forward or stumble backwards as I ride my orgasm down, grunting the final pulses of cum out. It dwindles to humming muscles and a quiet mind.

Nuzzling, I kiss her hair and then pull the toothbrush up to my mouth, deciding to see what Shoshanna and mint taste like. I brush my teeth again.

She rolls her eyes.

CHAPTER FIVE

7ᵗʰ Month

I moan as Clay takes me gently but with a thorough domination and a deep understanding of my body.

His appetite for me, and I for him, is insatiable, incessant... indecent. We can't get enough. Even as I swell around my hips with his babies, he only seems to want me more often.

Gentler, *yes*.

But just as consuming.

Placed and positioned on my side at the edge of the mattress, with my knees tucked high, I spoon the large white pillow to my torso as he thrusts and strokes.

God, he's deep.

The luxurious pillow is soft and soothing as he moves in and out of my arse and plays his fingertip along the wet folds of my pussy.

Takes his time.

Watches the show.

He's completely naked, broad chest spanning out as he holds me down with one powerful arm. A grid of abdominal muscles leads down to his thick cock.

He's lethal in the most beautiful and alluring way.

The devil would be more stunning than any other creature; he is to draw you in willingly before sinking through your skin to devour your soul.

Well, Clay Butcher can devour any part of me he wishes to, and I'll open for him to take and take.

The sight, sensation, and pressure overpower me, and I moan from in my throat.

"That's it, my sweet girl." His voice is a raspy, delicious timbre that pours over me like warm liquid. "Remember to breathe as I take this special part of you."

I do as he orders.

Pant.

Thrust.

God.

"Little deer, you're so very sweet like this." His fingertips strum down my quivering pussy. "Needy for my cock. Taking me in your pretty arse but wanting me desperately inside your wet pussy." The groan that leaves him rumbles against my backside as his pelvis meets my flesh. "*Christ.* You take every inch *here.*"

He trails his fingers down to the base of my spine. "Arch for me." His hand presses my lower back, coaxing my body to bow to an angle he likes. "Good girl. Show me how lovely your body looks when you bow."

I bury my face in the pillow when he pauses, entirely sheathed inside me. Feeling his eyes roaming my body, I will myself not to squeeze his cock, but the need to do so is a howl of demand in my mind.

"*Sir,*" I cry out as he pulses, taking mere inches out only to push back inside again and again.

He coos, "That's my good girl. Steady. You're so well-behaved for me. You're so perfectly-trained and stretched. Are you breathing, my sweet girl? Show me your lips."

My mind skitters from the pressure moving up and into me, but I do as I am told. Pulling the pillow down to my chin, I part my lips over the top of it and breathe deeply for him.

"Swollen lips. Just like your pussy. Like your little arsehole, like your stomach. All your pretty parts plump because of me, because of what I do to your body."

"*Yes.*"

The tiny strums of his fingers on my pussy have me rocking into them. Desperate to be filled. I know if he only slides them inside me, I will combust. I will explode.

"More," I beg. "More, Sir."

"Manners, sweet girl."

I whimper, saturated in desire. "*Please.*"

"Very good." He slides two fingers inside me with such accuracy and care, I can't withhold my groan of appreciation.

"What a lovely sound, little deer."

A darkened world scattered in stars hit my vision. I love being pregnant. Everything is more intense. Higher. Lower. Louder. Sorer. Sweeter. Deeper. I rock on his fingers, fucking myself as he thrusts in and out in a harder, determined way.

I grip the pillow, receiving his thorough penetration in both holes in completely contradictory ways. The hard, deep thrusts in my arse have him growling while his fingers stay steady and gentle and everything I need. It's hard to know where to focus, but I let him take me unabated—the way *he* needs.

"So wet. So tight. My young fiancé with her perfect pussy lips that love my tongue and cock and want to be played with all day long. So spoilt and greedy."

I am.

I squeeze my eyes shut and take his fingers, his words, his cock—*I am.*

No more than two minutes later, I'm humping his hand, my pussy clinging to his thrusting fingers as I come apart, and I can't relax... Can't. God. *Please.* I can't relax. I squeeze my arse around his cock, earning me a hiss from his lips.

"*Christ,*" he bites out but continues to puncture that special place through my orgasm, through my moans and my writhes, until he loses rhythm to our violent shudders.

Loses control to his dark need.

As I plunge into an abyss of pleasure, he reaches for the nape of my neck with one hand and grips hard so he can knock me up the bed with his drives. It happens fast.

Wave after wave of pleasure suffuses me, but I force my eyes open to watch him fall apart. It's my favourite thing. My thing. Only mine.

He comes inside me, heat erupting around his cock. I am in heaven when he comes. He might be the devil, but his dark pleasures are everything I ever wanted.

He leans back, dropping his head between his shoulder blades, and groans through the last pulses, wringing his cock out inside my arse.

The warmth of his cum offers relief from the friction, the stillness allows me a moment of reprieve, and I catch my breath as he fights to control his.

"Very pretty," he praises, lifting his head to look down at me through a heated blue gaze. "Even as I defile you, you're always so pretty. My pretty little queen. Let's clean you up."

He edges from inside me, and I cry out.

He stops. "*Easy.*" Distracting me from the way his wet length slides from inside my arse, he leans down and gives me a searing kiss. Instantly, I release the pillow and grip his taut shoulders to accept his mouth and tongue.

A simple thing.

A kiss.

It's everything.

And I get lost in it.

With his lips on mine, he lifts me from the mattress and walks with me into the shower, where he cleans every inch of me and spoils me a little more with his tongue.

In the dressing room, he prepares for the day, choosing a suit and tie, but watches me wander naked as I decide what to wear from the hundreds of outfits I have.

I pull out the white poplin dress Aurora chose for me months ago and touch the lace on the sleeves. My mother used to make things from old pieces of lace.

She would stitch dreamcatchers and tapestries. Once, when I was very little, I wanted to be a cat, like all children play at, and she made me lace glove-like paws. She then left me to play as a cat and drink milk, and I didn't see her for several hours... It is hard, even when I reach for the memories, they always end in her leaving.

Still, she was my mum. I smile at the memory of her, my hand finding the taut skin over my swelling stomach.

"Sweet girl?"

My smile spreads wider still at his supernatural-like ability to catch my emotions. "If we have a girl," I say to the garment before turning to face him. "Can we call her Ashlee? After my mother?" His perfectly masculine face softens on me. I amble towards him, saying, "And..." When I reach him, he cups both my cheeks in a way that suggests he wants to cradle every part of me. Hold me. Study me. I crane my neck to hold his attention. "You should name him if he's a boy."

He drags his thumb across my lower lip, playing with the soft flesh. "If you give me a girl, we will name her Ashlee, and if you give me a boy, he will be Luca."

After his father.

I like it. "And if I give you two girls?"

"You won't." He watches his finger explore my lip. "Butcher's very rarely have girls, little deer. Kelly is the first for three generations."

"You Butcher Boys are powerful swimmers."

A hint of a smile tugs at his lips. "Indeed."

CHAPTER SIX

max

I've known a lot of dirty bastards in my life. I grew up surrounded by them. They didn't have what I have.

A man has no place until he is living for her. He's lost, but worse still, he doesn't know it. He's aimless. All until his eyes have a focus—her. His actions serve her. His body protects hers. His mind replays her smile.

Cassidy...

My wife.

And the peace she has given me.

Peace and placemats, she calls it.

Beside me, my daughter breathes deeply in her sleep. Her eyes flicker beneath thin skin. When she's like this, she looks like my wife, and when she opens her grey eyes, mine stare back at me, and I know—I know this little child is mine.

I'll never forget the first moment I saw her in the flesh. She was already a toddler—I missed her entire life as a baby. She was... I sigh roughly. All thin blonde hair, all hopeful—*all her mum*—but for those eyes. The same ones that glossed over, gazing up at me like a hero.

A damn hero fresh out of prison...

Then she said, "Daddy." She knew me. *Of* me. I wasn't a stranger to her. She didn't blame me for my absence—I deserved all her contempt, but it never came. And I didn't know a heart could ache without pain until that moment.

I kiss her soft crown.

She settles fast most nights.

I could leave sooner than I do, but I can never bring myself to do it. Not until she is so deep, she won't feel me leave her... I can't bear the thought of her watching me leave her— I clear my throat.

With her tucked beside my body, her little head on my bicep, and golden hair in two plaids down her chest, she's nothing short of everything. Like her mother is. How these two perfect creatures came to be mine, I don't know. But the part of me that despises everything I am and have done can't help but fear they'll be taken away from me.

It scares the shit out of me. Losing either of them, I just wouldn't—I'd follow them to the gates and wait outside in the cold just to be close.

"Daddy?" she murmurs sleepily, stilling my thoughts before they bury me.

I keep my voice low. "Yeah?"

"Why is the ground hard? When I fall it hurts."

I stare at the stars projected on her ceiling and answer her seriously. "The earth is made of rock."

But I wish it was cottonwool for you.

Wish for never-ending softness.

This is just like her. Waking to ask a question attached to a dream or memory from the day, only to fall back asleep moments later. The entire world is new. Everything has a question mark when you're a child.

"But why did the builders make it like that?"

"Because rock is stable."

"Stables? Like for horses?"

"Stable means you can count on it to be what you need," I state, that familiar sense of place and purpose deep in my veins. A purpose Cassidy gave me—a man who was so lost before. I am this little girl's guide into the world. Her protector. Her *stability*. I'm the one to watch her experience and learn for the first time… at least for a while. She is mine.

But Cassidy, my wife, she is mine forever.

My first love.

My last breath will be loving her.

Missing my wife all of a sudden, I look at the door and concern for her rolls through my muscles. I ram it down because she's asleep—safe. I know this, but—

I crack my jaw.

"What's wrong, Daddy?"

Deflecting, I add, "What if the ground was made of balloons? What then?"

She giggles, and my concern lessens against the sweet sound. I did that. Not really known for my humour, but this little girl thinks I'm fucking hilarious. Even when I'm a moody prick, she giggles at me.

"We'd all be bouncing around and bumping into each other." She tucks herself in closer to my side. "It'd be fun, Daddy, but how would we eat or drink? We'd make a big mess everywhere."

I chuckle once. "True."

"And if it was made of sand, we'd sink."

"Also true."

"So…" she ponders, sorting the information out for herself. "The ground has to be hard even if we fall over and it hurts because it's *stable* and we can count on it, and we don't just bounce around making a mess?"

I press my lips to her forehead, preferring her thoughts and voice to my own. "You tell me."

"I think..." She makes a small humming sound before declaring, "I think, yes. The ground has to be hard."

"There is your answer."

"I'm really *smarter...*" Her words turn to a yawn, and several drawled consonants that trail her to sleep.

When her breathing becomes heavy, I slide out of her bed and leave her room.

Nodding at Carter, a man whose face would scare any monster under my daughter's bed, I leave him at his post outside her door.

Back in my room, I see Cassidy under the covers, taking up a small portion of the bed. I map her shape under my gaze. She is curled in, holding her pregnant stomach. My hand twitches to hold him, too. Place my hand over him so he can feel my affection through that action.

By the time I've showered and slid into bed, I'm ready to hold my world in my hands and go to sleep. But Cassidy's scent thickens my cock up to my navel.

I groan—fucking hell. Ignoring it, I cover her spine with my body and band my arm over her, cover my boy with my palm, and hold his mother as closely as I can.

Beneath my hand, I feel him move. It's not the first time I've felt it, but it has the same effect on me. My stomach, my world, caves in until I'm short on breath. I press back to let him know I'm here. I'll always be here.

"Please, Max."

My eyes flash open, but I don't move a muscle until I know exactly where she is, so I don't roll on her or elbow her—don't hurt her.

She's laying on me, her lips trailing softly down my throat, and... *fuck me*. I'm aching to come.

My cock woke up before me.

Or never fell asleep.

"Little one." I lift my arm to touch her, but can't. Tilting my chin upward, I meet the culprit of my restraint—her ballet tape circling my wrist and strapped to the headboard.

My body floods with heat.

It's dangerous how much I want to sink my cock into her, have her swallow and suck me in.

I'll tear her in two.

She's so fucking fragile, but she doesn't see it. She's lost weight since being pregnant, and there was nothing of my ballerina to start with.

"I can snap that tape in a second."

"But you won't," she whispers against my skin, crawling down, her pregnant belly touching me as she goes.

Cassidy doesn't wait for me to wake up completely, wrapping her mouth around my cock and swallowing the length, her tongue undulating against the vein pulsing underneath.

Fuck.

Reaching back with my free hand, I grip the headboard and wrestle with my muscles to not take her like a feral animal.

We haven't had sex in months. I can't. I can't risk hurting her, but— *God-fucking-dammit*, she groans around my cock, the vibrations filling my veins. *She* fills my veins. And I want her there.

She takes me to the back of her tongue, gags, and I both want to shove myself deeper and pull out to check she's breathing. But...

Fuck me, her mouth feels good.

With my unrestrained hand, I reach down and stroke her

throat as she works me hard, fast, a greedy sucking that has my head burning up and my body shaking through the effort to control my feverish impulse.

Stay in fucking control, Max, you arsehole.

I flex my hips, fucking into her mouth, but she stops and my cock slides along her tongue and out. My balls ache from the withdrawal, but now she is scampering up my body.

Don't you fucking dare, little one.

Growling, I rip my wrist free from the headboard, snapping the fabric easily but not fast enough because she's spread her white thighs over me, lowering herself onto my cock, and... *Goddammit*, the fucking relief of being inside her blinds me for a moment.

A perfect moment.

A moment of solace.

A moment I don't despise myself quite as much.

Then I growl, possessing her hips to stop her from taking another inch inside her delicate body. I look down. Her pussy, stretched and open, is a pink ribbon banding my cock. She is halfway down. Her mouth is open, panting, and the corners are ticked in a smile of utter relief.

"Max," she whimpers, squeezing my cock, forcing a consuming pleasure to dot my eyes. She dances halfway down my length, her hips rolling and circling. She's going to fuck me whether I hold her here or not.

"Little one," I warn.

"Let me, Max. I'll stop if I need to, I promise." She sounds husky as she chokes the ever-loving fuck out of me, taking more of my length inside her, and I— I let her. Releasing her hips, she edges down.

"One more inch," she says softly, shuddering. Then cries out as she takes another, and I clench my jaw as she sucks me deep. "Two." She fills herself with my cock. "Three. Four..." She goes on breathlessly.

My breathing is fierce. Once her pussy meets my pelvis, her mewling comes from somewhere so deep I feel the sound vibrating around my cock.

Naughty little ballerina.

I stare at her through my lashes, ready to fucking devour her, and she squirms against the intentions I feel set ablaze in my eyes; I still intimidate my wife.

"You're a naughty girl." I hold her smooth round belly with one hand, protecting him, keeping his safety present while I lose my mind in her body. Sliding the other up, I possess her throat to hold her in place, "You wanted this," I buck up, hitting her depths, forcing a yelp through her sweet lips. "You want my cock shoved inside you? Huh? You like me stretching you open? Tainting your purity? Show me what my little ballerina looks like when she's impaled on my huge cock."

"Max," she breathes, nervousness pitching her voice.

She steadies herself on my chest and starts to ride me in the smooth, sensual way only my tiny dancer can do—with grace and elegance. Like she is performing for me.

For me.

Only me.

She flushes. "Oh, *God.*" She rocks over me, trembling. "You're everywhere. I can feel you everywhere."

My little piece of innocence, sucking my cock into her pussy, demanding my length inside her, pretending to pin me down when we both know I could stop this... I could have.

Fuck.

Soon, with her pretty body and her sensual motion, she takes me to a place of peace. I need this. Whereas I always imagined I drag her down to the darkness with me, but I'm wrong—*was* wrong. As she sways on top of me, her eyes glued to mine, soft and in love, her pregnant belly rolling with her sensual movements, I realise she's guiding me out of the dark to meet her in the light.

"I love you, Max," she whispers, and my heart contracts so hard I can barely breathe through the sensation.

I squeeze her throat to show her how I feel. She's already nearly there, working herself faster, moaning as she drags upwards, and crying out as she rolls down again. Her pussy opens and holds me.

"*Max!*" Her orgasm is my name as she asks for my support in that breathy plea.

"I've got you, little one." I sit up, try not to crush her stomach, and hold her as she shakes against me.

Fuck me.

Look at her...

Pretty open lips. Freckles bunched at the bridge of her nose. Golden eyes glossy with pleasure.

My Cassidy Slater.

As her pussy ripples around my shaft, wringing pleasure up from the aching balls, demanding my cum, I see darkness, then... I throw my head back and growl, climaxing in a rush, pumping my cock into her tight wet channel, filling her with me, just like she fills every inch of my sanity with her.

"I win," she pants, cupping the back of my neck and dropping her forehead to mine.

"I'll destroy the competition, little one."

"You are my biggest competition. You and your guilt. I see the hate in your eyes, Max. I see the regret. I'll win over that feeling, too. Your demons will lose, Menace. I'm a really scary person," she says through a giggle.

Goddammit.

That sound.

I'll be your hero, little one.

CHAPTER SEVEN

clay

Our men take Aurora's luggage down the marble steps to the three waiting cars. The entire house is bustling with the move, and Aurora busies herself to combat the emotion she surely feels.

That I feel, too.

This stunning woman has been my twin pillar since I was born. But this is not my decision to make. I consider her my oldest, most precious friend, but her affections lay with other women and mine with only one—Fawn.

Aurora married me all those years ago to cement her place in the *Cosa Nostra*, the only way allowed—by being my wife. For my little deer, we broke our vows. We risked her position in the Family; the divorce went through a week ago.

And she is no longer beholden to me, to the District, but her heart still beats true for the *Cosa Nostra*. She wanted it more than even I. She wanted it like her father did, with a single-minded sense of place and purpose.

Which is why, the Godfather, our Don in Sicily, Alceu, has rightly acknowledged her loyalty and abilities. "Were she born with a cock, *se*, you may be dead, my boy," he had said to me on the phone several weeks ago.

He's probably right.

We may have been rivals, in lieu of joining our houses. We may not have fallen into the same roles or developed the same respect...

We will never know.

But alas, Alceu has given her a place at his side—his right side. A woman. It is unheard of, but for Aurora—for my ex-wife—exceptions are made, rules are bent, and men who defy this new world will find death fast.

She's just as ruthless as me.

More so, perhaps.

A woman does ruthless deeds in a very different way to a man; I am certain she will impress the Family in Sicily. She is taking her sisters with her, where they will be under her guidance and protection.

And from afar, I will always be her ally.

Her friend.

I smooth my tie down my shirt as she approaches me, her dark hair perfectly straight down her back, her skin a warm olive glow that radiates not only beauty but power. "You're not going to miss me, are you, Clay?"

A smile hits my lips. "Missing you will not change your mind. It is a brilliant waste of my time, but yes, I still will."

She places her palm on my cheek. "We both have what we want now, Clay."

"Alceu is not long for this world, should you need my support when he go—"

"*Clay.*" She waves her hand at me, dismissive, and my smile widens further as she is the only person I truly see as my equal in all things. "I am going to rule over Sicily—my country."

"Yes," I agree because she will. I have no doubt she'll slice her way through the made-men in the Family for her place at the head when the time comes. "But should you need me."

"Then I will call."

A small whimper causes heat to hit my head and awaken my instinct to protect and serve. I turn to see my little deer staring at Aurora with the same sadness I feel but do not outwardly show.

I stare at her. "Sweet girl?"

Fawn looks at Aurora. "I don't want you to go."

"Fawn," Aurora coos, sashays towards her, and places a small kiss on either side of her cheek. "Do not cry for me. This is not because of you. You—" A gloss hits Aurora's whiskey-coloured eyes— "have given my Family stability. You have grounded an impossible man, and for that, you're a queen. The District only needs one." She lifts my little deer's chin. "Protect him," she says gently before turning to face me. "From his self-destructive isolation."

I smirk. "*Madonna Mia.*"

Aurora says to Fawn, "You need to be strong with him. Tell him what you want. What we spoke about. He may not always agree, but he will listen, and you are far more persuasive than you think."

Fawn tries to smile. "When will I see you again?"

"Well, I know you want to wait until after the birth of your children to set a date for the wedding. I understand you want to be free of pregnancy to truly enjoy all aspects of your wedding and honeymoon. I will be back for that."

"I thought you could be my maid of honour."

"I would. It would be my privilege to do so; however, I thought, perhaps…" Aurora brushes a piece of blonde hair over Fawn's shoulder, and Fawn sighs, clearly liking the affection. "I could give you away."

Fawn inhales with delight.

It occurs to me at this moment that Aurora has taken on a motherly figure to my little deer. The affection was misplaced before, when I thought she wanted a female lover, but was seemingly desperate for a mother. I suppose for a young girl who knew no love or stability from a woman, where to place affection might be confusing.

My little deer's eyes fill with tears. "Yes, please."

"I will see you for that very important task."

She leaves Fawn's side after a small embrace and approaches me. Her elegant, smooth demeanour only lightly conceals the emotion of leaving her city and confidant.

I look down at her. "I am proud of you."

She lifts to her toes and kisses both my cheeks. "I am proud of you."

Without another word of sentiment, she turns on her heels, strides down the waterfall of steps, and climbs into the backseat of the idling Chrysler.

Her driver leads a convoy of cars away from her family home, from the house she grew up in, without sadness. I know Aurora. She will brush a single tear that dares escape, not for the house or the District, purely for a part of her life now concluded, before smiling at the opportunities ahead of her.

I turn to see my sweet girl with tears streaming down her cheeks and falling from an adorable wobbling chin. "I'm worried about her," she says. "What if they are mean to her."

"I would be far more concerned about the men in Sicily that think her simply a woman." I loosen my tie at my collar. A sudden urge to have my little deer suck my cock rushes heat along my skin. It's her tears, the trembling lip, her concern. It makes me want to please her, redirect her attention, and show her our bond. Teach her about *my devotion* to her body.

She shuffles her feet under my gaze. "I know that look, Sir." Her throat rolls as she swallows over a lump. "I have something I have to ask you, can I? I have to do it now."

Studying her, her finger twirling her long blonde hair by her waist, I recognise uncertainty in her mannerisms and recall Aurora's words from moments ago: *"Tell him what you want. What we spoke about."*

"Use your voice, sweet girl."

Squaring her shoulders, she walks towards me. A big blue eye and a doe-like green one lock on me with severity, her neck craning when she stops at my feet. "I want a home birth, Sir." She nods to further press her statement. "I want to have our babies under the moon, in a bath, with a midwife. No doctors. Just us and the magic of the world. I don't want them to be a number on a board when they are born. Or have a tag on their wrist. I've been a name on a file my whole life. *Please.*"

Christ.

Impossible.

Finding her chin, I take hold of her and brush my thumb over her lower lip. The image of her mouth open and saliva dripping around my cock slides into my mind. I get harder. "I know I swore to give you everything you ask for, but not at the expense of your safety. The only time I will deny you anything will be under that premise. I will not allow anything short of the best care under the eyes of the best doctors in the country. My answer is no, sweet girl."

She tears up, and I clench my teeth to abate the need to retract my statement. I cannot choose her happiness over her safety. Will not.

"I don't like hospitals," she says weakly.

I despise the meek volume of her lovely voice, so I try to soothe her. "I will be there the entire time. Safety comes first, little deer. Share the moon, your magic, with our children after their birth."

She chews on her lower lip, probably tasting the salt of her own sorrow. A sting to match my words. I'll fix this. I need to make her come, to spoil her for pleasure. Remind her how I'll please her, but for this, I can't falter.

Less than ten minutes later, I'm on my back and pulling her down to sit on my face, the scent of her sensual skin engorging my cock to the point of pain, making it throb with its own heartbeat.

"Fuck," I bite out a growl, covering my mouth and nose with her sweet pussy. I look up to see the lower curve of her swollen stomach; the pretty sight rips another groan from me.

I like her pregnant.

I glide my tongue up and down her slit, chasing the ripples of her need as her skin reacts to my attention. She grinds on me.

Christ, sweet girl.

That's it.

Sit on my tongue.

Breathing through my nose, I single-mindedly suck and lick her to a shuddering mess. I gorge on her orgasm, lathering my tongue with her, wrenching more of her climax from her greedy little pussy.

I need more of her.

Though she is all over me, inside my soul, fuelling my heart and directing my body, I want more of her. My sweet girl—the one person in the world who handles my evil.

When I don't stop as she shudders the remains of her pleasure away, her moans become a perpetual whimper. I don't let up. I lick and suck her until her muscles can no longer hold her upright.

After I lay her down to sleep, I'm kept from slumber by our earlier conversation. Her dreamcatcher sways slightly by the bedpost, reminding me how these ideals are part of her passions. Of her humanity.

But a doula is not a doctor.

A home birth is archaic, impractical—*Christ.*

I turn to watch her sleep, heavy blonde lashes lay over her flushed cheeks, and she stuns my heart to a stop.

I love her.

There has never been a more lovely sight. I do not believe in her spirituality, but I believe in her. *Still…* her safety must always come first.

CHAPTER EIGHT

shoshanna

9TH MONTH

Everything hurts.

Being pregnant really tests my tolerance. I wouldn't call myself an overly accepting person to start with; add a cocktail of estrogen and other pregnancy players, and I'm as temperamental as a lioness being woken up too early.

The sun blazes above us and green peppermint trees line the street. Thin leaves reach out, creating canopies that offer the footpaths shade.

I hold my large stomach as we walk the District Boulevard. My black dress flows over the mound.

It was my idea to head out for a sense of normalcy, to get an ice cream and some sun, but my swollen feet and whale-like physique are making me regret it.

Majestic? Like hell.

We're winding down.

Baby will be here soon.

I look down at Stone, waddling.

Same, kiddo.

He holds my hand while in the other an ice cream dribbles over his skin. Smiling, I remind myself this is for him. We may not have much more time with just the three of us. Things will change, but that's okay. I just know it can be hard on a firstborn.

I look over Stone to Bronson, who devours his cotton-candy-flavoured ice cream with the same enthusiasm his rumbustious son does. Both of them—*nutcases.* Purple and pink cream slides down the waffle to his inked fingers.

A man is ahead of us, moving fast and not looking down to see we have a toddler between us. When he bumps Stone, he mutters a grunt of an apology but continues on his course.

I freeze up as Stone stares at his ice cream, now upside down on the concrete, the rainbow colours mingling into a stream of sludge.

Just as Stone's eyes well up, Bronson hands him his cone. Stone beams. He has a quick turnaround, that kid. Just like his dad. Knowing what is coming, I scoop Stone up and walk in the opposite direction to Bronson.

Stopping a few meters ahead, I turn back to watch my six-foot-five tattooed, borderline insane lover stalk the man down the footpath and push him through a shop window.

Just. Like. That.

As casual as a pat on the back.

Leaning in through the window now bordered by broken glass needles, Bronson casually says, "Must have slipped on ice cream, mate."

The shopkeeper gasps but doesn't approach. She knows who Bronson Butcher is. The man on the floor shakes with confusion. Bronson offers him his hand, helping him back through the glass like he didn't just shove him through it. The man blinks at the sidewalk, a haze of uncertainty in the slow batting of his lashes. The "what just happened" is evident in his wide, searching gaze.

Bronson brushes off the man's shirt before ambling back towards me with a smirk on his lips and a single dimple displayed that gentrifies his mischievous nature.

He's actually pleased with himself.

I suppose for Bronson, that was a mild response to the situation. He reaches me. "Don't worry, baby. I'll send Mrs Pannell some money for the window in the morning."

His grin causes my insides to flip around. "Put your dimple away," I order, shaking my head as he joins my stride, and we continue down the sidewalk.

We don't get far before I suddenly feel like I need to pee, and then water slides down my legs and pain shoots through my abdomen.

Placing Stone down, I keel over and hold my stomach as cramps bear down around my pelvis like a vice squeezing me.

"Fuck," I mutter.

"Baby?" Bronson's voice reaches me inside the pain fog, but I can't move a muscle against the onslaught of the contractions.

God, this is fast.

Within a moment, I'm swept into his arms, and he's walking with me inside a coffee shop and sitting me in a booth.

"Call us an ambulance, quickly, like a bunny." I hear him say, provoking a young girl to rush out of sight, and he's back facing me. His eyes trained and ready. I try to focus.

Stone?

Where is Stone?

I wince. *"Stone."*

"Mummy?" His sweet voice answers my question, but I can't talk or see straight or focus—*God.*

"Stone, you have a really important job, little buddy. You ready to be a big brother?"

He nods. "Yes, Daddy."

"Good. You're on watch. Lord Commander of the Ambulance Watch." Bronson points to the glass doors. "Sit right next to the door and wait for the ambulance. Don't take your eyes off the road. Got it?"

"Got it!" Stone plonks down outside the door, in clear view of us both but far enough away to blind him to the sight of me and what is happening very fast.

I close my eyes and breathe.

Bronson strokes his fingertips down my face, along the bridge of my nose and down to the bow of my lips. "I'm here, my beautiful Shoshanna. I'm here."

Time passes, but the contractions are rolling together, too intense, and the medical professional in me knows we don't have much time.

Fuck.

I wriggle my knickers down. Bronson grabs them and stuffs them into his back pocket. I'd curse at him—I'd demand these ones actually get returned, but I'm in too much pain.

Gritting my teeth, I reach between my thighs and push my fingers inside. I widen my legs and thrust upward to find my cervix. I moan through the pain of being in this position while birth spasms roll along my spine.

Finally, I feel my end.

I'm already dilated.

One finger, two fingers, three, four, five, I keep counting and measuring the space until my pulse ignites on the final number. My fingertips skate over the top of our baby's scalp, and…

Fuck.

He's coming.

Soon.

"I'm going to give birth here." I grab Bronson's arm and pull him between my legs. "Help."

"*Fucken, ay*. Okay, baby. I've got you." He slides his fingers inside me, replacing mine. "I've got you both."

"You need to guide him out." I groan, my head rolling back on the booth wall. "If you can—" I clench my teeth. "Hold his body and protect him; he'll be— Weak—"

"You remember when I felt you here for the first time? We were like sixteen. At the lookout," he reminds me, distracting me. "You squeezed me, and I thought you were the most incredible creature. Your body. I was in awe of how it worked. How *you* worked."

He keeps talking as a contraction rips a cry from me, damn near crippling me. I growl and push until it stops, feeling the birth happening right now into Bronson's hands.

Holy, fucking, fuck.

The pain!

"I'm still in awe of everything you are, baby," he says, green eyes shining bright and fiercely for me, for volatility. His emotions are always on display in the green hue of his eyes. "What you can do, my beautiful distraction. How you look after us— Stone, me."

The pangs of pain are immersive, dragging me down and making his words hard to hear. Shooting up my spine, wrapping around my back, flaring through my temples, no.

"*No. No. No.*" I shake my head and cry.

Bronson cups my cheeks and kisses my tears away, demanding each one for himself. "You're a warrior. You're the toughest, most badarse woman I know."

He looks down between my legs. The sensations there are conflicting and confusing. I don't know what he sees, but he looks fucking impressed and excited, and I want to whack that childlike glee off his face.

And kiss him hard for it, too.

"You're so close," he says, his voice deep. "Push for me, baby. Push that little bit of me, and that little bit of you, out."

My shoulders shake as I sob, remembering the seventeen-year-old version of Bronson Butcher bouncing on the mattress with his feet on either side of my body, calling out to the world with pride lacing his voice, "We are having a baby!"

"We made a life, Shoshanna!" He laughs, bouncing to his feet, planting them on either side of my body. "We made a life. And he won't be angry or sad or broken." His grin breaks his face, consumed by happiness. He starts to cry. "He'll be perfect. 'Cause you are. And I'll learn to be, baby. I swear it. I'll be better. A good citizen. Pay taxes and shit. I'll get a part-time job or whatever. Fuck, I'll work on bikes. I'd like that." He stares into my eyes as I try not to cry. Not to join his wild happiness that isn't rational or mature but instead hopeful, and so Bronson. "I'll cook dinner for you every damn night," he says. "We'll never eat in front of the TV. We'll sit at the table and talk about our day. I'll sit at the head, and you'll sit beside me, and he'll make a mess on the floor, but the dog will clean it up—"

"The dog?"

"Yeah. A staffy. And it'll be fucking perfect."

The vision floods me, and I tense through my shoulders and squeeze my teeth together. Pushing hard until a flood of weight drops from my pelvis, I bear down.

The pain dwindles.

A gurgling cry draws me back to the moment, so I open my eyes to the most spectacular vision. A boy with a head full of dark hair. Tears stream down Bronson's face as he checks the boy over while I reach down between my legs. I'm not bleeding too much, very little, actually.

He lifts the boy out in front of him, only slightly as the

cord still joins us, and—*oh my God*—he bellows out the theme song for *The Lion King.*

I want to kill him.

But I don't.

He can do that, act animated in the serious moments and make me want to melt and murder him at the same time.

I laugh, cry, and will myself not to close my eyes against the exhaustion because I don't want to miss this. The smile. The crying. The theatrics. It's my Nutcase. The boy that sings to my soul, the man who has one half of my heart.

Too soon for this moment and too late for the previous, the ambulance officers burst through the door and drop down beside us, and I can finally relinquish my medical hat and let them take it from here.

I can relax.

While they check the bub.

While they check me.

I can relax.

My head hits the back of the booth again, and through hooded eyes, I watch Bronson show his boy off to the paramedics with a huge grin etched across his masculine face.

"Look what my baby made? He's perfect. Another Butcher, alright." He waves Stone over. "Look at your brother, Stoney. What do you think of all that hair?"

Stone peers over Bronson's shoulder, almost disgusted by the gooey bub. "So hairy!"

Bronson laughs. "Like a werewolf!"

"Like a Butcher," I whisper softly, and Bronson's turquoise eyes lock on me. They scream, "I love you."

A serene smile touches his mouth, the contentment running deep into his soul.

"Our boy," he states, holding my gaze.

I smile. "Our boy."

CHAPTER NINE

cassidy

9ᵀᴴ MONTH

I writhe in pain.

It's been hours.

I always intended to have a natural birth, just like I did with Kelly, but the contractions are coming on hard and fast, and my cervix refuses to open.

I curl over, holding the outside of my swollen belly while convulsions tumble through my pelvis. I can feel Max's dangerous energy on the edge of explosion, so I reach out and grip his hand. He drops to his haunches and kisses my face, lips, cheeks, eyes, all over the tears.

"It is time, Mr Butcher," Dr Shen implores. "We have applied the induction gel directly to her cervix; it should have worked by now. She is not dilating, and she's in pain."

"No!" Max booms, snapping his head towards the doctors. They freeze up as Max rises, my hand slipping from his, his body towering over the staff. He cares little for them. I know this. He's not a bad person, but he'll do bad things if he feels cornered. This is the epitome of Max Butcher cornered. "Do you have a death wish? You're not cutting my wife open!"

I reach out my hand and grip his tattooed forearm, capturing his attention like gravity. He's ready to be there with his actions and attention. A position I can rely on.

I stare into his gaze. "It'll be okay." My voice is weak, but I'm not. I can endure this pain. I've danced on broken toes before, but it's the unknown that frightens me. "I'll be okay. Let's get our baby out *now*."

Max is shaking his head at me, pain darkening his eyes, the dread of trusting someone to touch me with a knife carved into tempestuous grey depths. "I know, Menace." I nod, understanding him. "Hold my hand," I say, my voice choked with distress, my throat tightening against the threat of more tears. "Please."

"If they hurt you—"

"I'll be okay." I blink a few tears through my lashes. "It's less painful than last time. It's safer for him and *me*. Trust the doctors, Menace."

"I don't trust anyone with you."

"I know."

I hold Max's attention in a way that blocks out the world. Whereas he's on the edge of murder, he's still my Max, and he keeps me anchored to him while the doctors sit me up, insert the needle into my spine, and lay me down again.

And they cut me.

I'm not sure where I am while they do it, lost somewhere safe in Max's grey-blue gaze. Nothing can hurt me when he's close. And although he doesn't break eye contact with me, I know he's paying attention to everything the doctor does. His predator-like watch playing out in the violent pulsing of his jaw muscles.

Tugging at my pelvis starts.

"Promise me you'll grab our baby straight away, Max." My

shaky voice draws him closer to me. He presses his forehead to mine, our eyes inches apart. "Promise me because I won't be able to move until they finish stitching me up."

He nods stiffly against my brow.

The jerking at my hips is all I feel. Max's eyes are all I can see, up close and wild. The tiny grey freckles and big black pupils would terrify anyone who knew what they had planned should anything go wrong— Suddenly, those two senses dissolve with the sound of a husky cry.

A cry that gets louder.

That's our baby.

Tears stream down my cheeks to my temples. "Get our baby, Max," I whisper quietly, and Max's head snaps to the side, chasing the sound instantly.

I thought he'd freeze up, thought he'd be wary, unsure, but he strides to the doctor and takes his baby into his hands, possessive and confident. I can almost see the words "mine" rippling through his muscles as he holds the tiny person in his hands, the floppy head in his palm, the wriggling back and bum in his other. Our baby fits entirely in Daddy's big hands.

This is the moment.

My heart pirouettes.

Weakly, I flop my head to the side as the doctor stitches me up. Seeing my Max roll his gaze over his baby for the first time, I cry happy tears and thank the world for every moment that ensured I had this one.

"It's a boy," the doctor announces to me, guiding a very guarded Max over to the table. To this day, he trusts no one with me, Kel, and now, with this little man. I used to think he'd lock me away in a tower if he could.

A boy.

A little Max Butcher.

I watch from the bed as the doctor clamps the umbilical cord and checks his mouth and chest. The lovely sight blurs behind rapid, happy tears. It's the most beautiful thing I have ever seen. It's the vision of my dreams.

It's what I wanted. Nothing like the last time when I was alone and in pain, pushing and pushing, screaming for Max to make me feel safe. I was still so young.

Fawn's age.

Max keeps a firm hold on his whimpering son. It's what he promised that day when he spoke to my stomach—that he would show our child how he feels about him the minute he was born.

I soak in the sight of Max Butcher as he approaches, bunched muscles that stretch the fabric around his biceps, a face full of awe as he stares at our son.

"He's incredible, little one," Max states, deep and possessive, lowering our baby boy so I can reach up and stroke his cheek. Our son pouts at the air, and I know I need to get him on me soon.

The rest of the room melts away again while I am stitched and checked, my eyes glued to Max, his flooded in wonder at our son.

A weak smile slides to my lips; fatigue and happiness play with my mood.

My hospital bed is wheeled to another room, and we are given some privacy, so Max lays our son on my chest. We lift the mattress until I am sitting, supported.

I play with his lips and try to get him to latch onto my nipple. It's familiar. Last time, I had a lactation nurse here, but it seems unnecessary for a second child unless they refuse to latch. I know what to do this time.

Feeling Max's eyes on me, I realise he's never seen me do this before. He never saw me breastfeed. "Kelly wouldn't latch for ages." I offer some insight, hoping he'll feel more included in this experience. "But..." I trail off as my little boy's mouth starts to suckle. It won't let-down just yet, but it will soon.

He'll make it happen. "He's going to do just fine. Typical boy."
I laugh, but I'm tired, so it's a little breathy. Max lowers his
lips to my forehead, kissing my skin.

Instantly, I miss Kelly.

It's a longing I get when she's away; all the little pieces that
make up Kelly are connected to me, like this baby is, like Max
Butcher is. *Our thing* is all four of us now.

"Kelly?" I say, my head hitting the mattress, and I rest my
eyes for just a moment.

"Daddy." I hear Kelly's voice, but I don't open my eyes yet,
breathing deeply in and out on the mattress. "Should I tell him
that I love him? Because I do."

"Sure."

I open my eyes to the sight of Max rocking our son back
and forth, and Kelly perched on the armrest with her feet in
her dad's lap. She looks down at her new little brother. "But
doesn't that mean something bad?" she asks innocently. "Like
I won't be showing him? Like I'm gonna leave or somethin'?"

"Hi," I breathe so they know I'm awake.

Max's eyes shoot to me, and I want to leap into his arms
and have him hold and kiss me, but my lower half still feels
numb, so that curbs my impulses.

"Little one," is all he says, but his tone is deep and adoring.
The way he says "little one" has always been reverent; a soul's
worth of love strained through each letter. He returns his gaze
to our daughter. "Kel, you should say whatever you want."
There is a pause while he searches her questioning gaze.
"Does it bother you? That I don't say it to you. Do you
understand why?"

"No." Her voice is dubious. "Yes. I don't know. You are a
horse's *stable*. Right?" I have no idea what she's talking about.

"That is what it means. You don't say it 'cause I can *count* on my fingers that you will be what I need? Right?"

I try not to laugh.

He sighs roughly, and then he says, "I'm stable, hard, too, like most stable things. I'm hard on myself. Love is too good for me. But it's not for you. I love you, Kel." My lower lip wobbles with happiness because I've never heard him say the words. Not once. I cover my mouth to hold the whimpering inside. "I love you immensely and completely," he declares. "You should hear the words. Not saying them was a promise I made your mum." His eyes hit mine, and I lower my hand so he can see my happiness. "A promise to never need to say them; I would always *show her*," he says to me, then returns his gaze to Kel. "Your mum and I were ripped apart for a time, and I found those words hard to say before I left. I was— I wasn't sure what they meant. I had a very different upbringing to you. I *still* find them hard to say—they are not enough. They fall short of what I feel for you three. But I don't want you to wake up one day and think my dad never told me he loves me. You should hear it. I love you, Kel."

"You deserve love, Max," I say to him.

"Yeah, Daddy. I love you."

A quiet smile touches Max's lips. "The words sound good." He looks down at his son, who sleeps soundly like a typical newborn. "I want him to be able to say them, little one. I don't want him to be like me."

"I do," I declare straightaway, and Max's grey-blue gaze returns to me, warming all the contradictory parts of me that love all the contradictory parts of him. "I hope he is exactly like you, Menace."

CHAPTER TEN

fawn

9TH MONTH

The sheets are cold. A jarring sensation given my pregnant body is otherwise prickling with warmth and drenched in perspiration.

In my hazy sleep state, I recall altering the air-conditioner last night, but I'm certain I didn't switch it off. I reach out, seeking Sir's hard, muscular form, but find his side of the bed empty but for a slight dip—a small patch where his body recently warmed.

Moaning, I slowly come to.

Awareness circles me in that moment; my toes, my body, all the parts of me hum to life, and I immediately sit up. Something feels different. I feel lighter—Yet, heavier at the same time. *Heavier... lower...*

Searching the room, I find the wall lights casting a dim glow below them and Clay's eyes locked on me as though viscerally fixed. Watching. Wait.

For what, Sir?

He's naked but for a pair of jeans sitting around his toned hips. "Little deer." His blue gaze softens on me, his concern smoothing to trained control.

Peering wide-eyed down at the sheets, I feel my heart contract. I clutch at it. Rub it. Without even seeing the mess, I know my lower half is wet.

"It's okay, sweet girl."

I barely hear him. A whimper thrashing from inside me because I've lost them—*again.* Panicked, I touch the damp blanket around my waist, gasping for air through my rising pulse. I'm hollow. I feel hollow.

Where are they?

Where are my babies?

I can't do this again.

What is wrong with my body!

Clay is upon me, cupping my cheeks before I have time to lift the sheets and assess the bloody damage that will—

"Calm down, sweet girl." His lips hover over mine. "Your water broke. The babies are fine."

"What?"

"You're in labour, little deer." He strokes my cheeks with his thumbs, gazing into my eyes dotingly. "Your water broke, Fawn. You're fine."

"They're,"—I clutch at our unborn children, covered in my skin and heavy against my uterus—"They're okay?"

Clay forces a smooth signature grin but is unable to mask his concerns. They are rooted in the love he has for me and his babies. Today is the day he loses control of the situation. Not only loses it, nope, but *relinquishes* it to another. To a doctor. And that is Clay Butcher's worst nightmare. If he could deliver the baby himself, I swear he would.

His tone is a deep, gravelly timbre as he says, "They are perfect. Are you able to stand, or shall I carry you?"

My eyes sweep the room. It's strangely still and

uncomfortably quiet, absent of the shambling of feet I had expected come L-Day.

It's time to leave, I suppose. To push. And meet our babies... I feel tears cling to the backs of my eyes. My throat clogs up with fear of the impending pain, fear I'll do something wrong—that *my body* will do something wrong...

And everyone will see.

A room full of strangers.

A hospital. Hating the idea of leaving the house yet, I consider stalling. If I stall, maybe they'll just shoot out like a bar of soap from a tight fist. The doctor could give Clay a cricket mitt, so he can catch them as they fly from inside me. I've heard stories—

Shaking my head, I draw myself out of my delusions. I'm just not ready to be a number on a chart; I've been a number on a chart my entire life. In foster care... that is all you are.

I don't want that right now. "Are we going to the hospital soon? Or can we wait a bit?"

"Not exactly."

My breath catches. "What?"

"Can you stand, or shall I carry you?" he repeats, dipping to kiss my nose, followed by my lips. It's soft. I have a different Clay Butcher today. Leaning back, he pins me with a honed focus. "I'd very much like to carry you."

The weight of our babies seems to push harder on my pelvis, so I nod. "But I'm wet. I don't want—"

My words are cut off when he threads his arm under my legs and braces my back and neck with his other. Lifting me with ease, he walks through the empty house.

Each corridor is bathed in a soft orange hue. The sound of Clay's confident rap along the floor is even and loud in the absence of other noise.

Where is everyone?

Henchman Jeeves.

Jasmine.

When I pictured L-Day, it was a calamity. The mansion hectic with activity, orders and formalities soaring through the corridors. Royals are born! Alert the corgis. Ring the bells. A soldier at every exit. Fireworks. A helicopter. All the X-men — I'm not sure what they are doing; maybe protecting me or carrying me, which seems a little strange—

My wild thoughts end when a mild pain rolls along my pelvis. I bury my face in Clay's chest, the beating of his heart against my ear is like a drum counting down with his footsteps. While outwardly he's... *Clay. Sir.* My rock of smooth, delicious control.

We approach the double French doors, and they open before us, so I lift my head to see two women, one whom I recognise as Justine—the midwife who I met before Clay chose an obstetrician.

But the doctor isn't here...

Not that I can see.

Just two nurses.

On the alfresco, near the spot I first sat and looked out over the gardens, they prepare towels and equipment beside a small ceramic wading pool.

My breath hitches.

He... didn't.

He said no.

The tears still hanging to the back of my eyes force their way out, rushing my face.

God, what is this?

The entire alfresco is glowing beneath the moon. A cloudless sky gifts us a black dome shimmering in stars.

"It goes against everything I am to take unnecessary risks," he states, lowering me to the ground and holding me until I'm steady on my feet, the pressure inside me dropping even lower. "And to risk you, to risk them, the premise was damn unacceptable. The decision was a simple one." He releases a rough sigh, and I arch my neck to better gaze into his glistening blue eyes. Like the stars. Like my everything. "But you used your voice, sweet girl." He smiles softly. "You told me what you wanted, and I refused you. It has pained me for some time. When I saw your water had broken, I started organising the night meticulously. I called the doctor. The hospital. Organised our driver.

"It was all very practical. I felt myself separating from the moment. Then you shuffled and caught my eye. In that second, my chest, little deer, it hurt so immensely to see you. Not from sadness, of course. And I found myself staring at you still sleeping, unaware. Peaceful. Your dreamcatcher hanging above your head." His voice tightens, his throat rolling over a lump. He's emotional. He's showing me... he's letting me see him. God, it's *perfect.*

"Not everything is practical," he states. "Love, quite frankly, is exceedingly impractical." He smiles smoothly, a real one, one that makes him look half his age. "But every damn thing that people say about being in love is true. It is the only reason we are here." He strokes my face. "*You* are the only reason I am here. I was wrong to deny you this, little deer."

Tears burst from me under his attentive gaze. "We're having a home birth, Sir?"

"Under the moon, sweet girl."

"But," I fumble for the words, thrown a little due to his adamance before that '*safety comes first, little deer. Share your magic with them later.*'

He goes on, "I may not believe in all the things you do, but I believe in *you*. And you're going to prove to me that magic exists when you show me what you made for me."

More tears wet my face, so I tease him, "And you have a convoy of cars ready, don't you, Sir? And a doctor on standby? The X-men, too?"

He *actually* laughs, deep and real and rumbles with the choke of his emotions. *It is everything.* His deep tone, the moment, the way his eyes are filling further with the glisten of tears. It's everything a girl like me dreams about and everything a girl like me deserves.

"I'm prepared," he states emphatically, amusement still circling his tone. "Let us leave it at that."

The birth begins with me wading and moving in the small paddling pool, breathing through the long, dull throbs.

The night has given us utter peace. A perfect stage. No machines beeping. No strangers hovering. A silent moment at our house, with Clay and I under the moonlight.

The overhead fairy lights reflect in the water, creating the illusion of my body moving through the stars. It's so pretty. So magical.

Clay sits beside me, watching with his hands clasped below his chin. If he could take the pain away, I know he would. He'd trade it. Burden someone else, anyone else, but it's not so bad, really. It's sweet agony, in a way.

Primal.

When the surges begin to consume me, I lay my forehead and arms over the edge of the pool so Clay's fingers can stroke through my hair. A fan of blonde floats around me.

"That's my sweet girl," Clay coos, his voice strained, hiding concern. "You're so brave. You're so strong."

I bury my sweaty face in my arms. Tensing, my body contracts—*God.*

Breathe...

I inhale and exhale through the pain.

"You remember, Fawn," Justine says as she steps into the pool to check how dilated I am. I spread my legs for her.

"Focus on your toes. When you feel the contractions, think, 'What are my toes doing?' Touch them to the bottom of the pool. You're safe. *Grounded.*"

I nod, exhaustion already clinging to my muscles.

She smiles. "It's time to help them. When you next feel one, I want you to push."

Clay steps into the water in his jeans, and I shuffle around until I am leaning against his firm bare chest. Feeling his steady breaths, I sigh into him.

Better than the ground.

I lock my jaw as a spasm twists along my lower half. Groaning, I push as hard as I can, but I don't focus on the ground or my toes. Don't focus on the moon or my breath. I concentrate on Clay Butcher's heart beating through my spine. The strongest, most powerful tempo in the world. The beat that holds me. That keeps me safe. That helps me push.

The pain is immense, everywhere and isolated at the same time. I push through it all.

My body loosens as baby number one leaves me; relief mixed with dread suddenly trails my groans to whimpers. Fatigued but feverish, I open my arms, waving them, needing her or him straight away. The baby's crying is lovely, high-pitched, delicate and *ours.*

Our baby.

I want...

The tiny human is pink and bloody and has so much damn hair. Dark hair, like Daddy. The baby is placed in my arms, against my chest, pulling the cord up from between my legs; we are still joined there.

Clay's hands circle me to cover mine… His hands on mine. Mine on our baby. *On our boy.*

Him...

A boy...

Luca.

"Time to push again," Justine says, but I'm not ready. I want to stare longer, map every little wrinkle, each strand of hair. Luca and I need time. She must read my expression, as she insists. "I can feel another little head."

The nursing assistant gently takes Luca from me, and I bear down on my teeth and push again. Tears spit from my eyes, but not really from the pain, from something entirely ineffable. A feeling so great and consuming and scary, it's simply ineffable.

I anchor myself on Clay.

He is my ground.

I cry as I push and push, though I want to slow down, but baby number two is being pulled from me, the feel of his legs leaving my body strange and... and...

It's over.

Now, Luca is placed with care on my left side and another... *boy*... on my right, tucked against my breasts, and they are both perfectly shaped little boys—little Butcher brothers with pouty lips and full heads of dark hair.

Two hands.

Five fingers each.

Moments pass as I catch my breath. Justine checks me over; my heart rate; my blood pressure are all fine.

Two feet.

Five toes each.

Thankfully, Justine moves ahead of time and the earth slows its spinning for me.

Two open eyes.

One button-shaped nose.

When I turn to lay sideways with my legs making a pyramid over Clay's thigh and my back held by his arm, it's just the four of us in the slow-motion world.

Under the moonlight, it's so still now. Everything else melts away. Clay's blue gaze drops to take in his keening little boys, and perhaps for the first time since I met him, he has nothing to say. No praises. Or encouragement. No words of wisdom. The sweet sight of his sons has rendered him speechless.

"They did so good, Sir," I say softly, while both boys quieten down, nuzzling into my sides. Barely feeling the aches through the endorphins and euphoria, I turn to face Clay so I can properly present him with his sons.

He accepts both boys, holding their heads in his palms, with their backs cradled along his tattooed forearms.

And just like that, he's a dad.

Not the Don of the *Cosa Nostra.* Not my Sir or the mayor or the most powerful man in the city, but something far more important and infinitely simpler.

Just a man.

A man holding his twin boys for the first time. A man with tears rushing over his chiselled jaw. With a smile—a genuine smile—the kind that lights up every inch of his face, that glows along each line. The kind that only comes around once in a while from a man like Clay Butcher.

"*Madonna Mia,*" he finally says, his voice overcome as his gaze sweeps over his perfect little heirs. "Look what your magic made for me, little deer."

CHAPTER ELEVEN

ten months later

LUCA BUTCHER

"Play gentle with my daughter, *se?*" I declare to my son Bronson, mild humour set into my tone.

I lean forward and grab my whiskey from the outdoor table. The ice clicks as I bring the amber liquor to my nose, inhaling what I can only describe as the scent of my life and business.

"It's our bit," Bronson calls over, pretending to mind my word before jerking back to push Cassidy into the pool with a smile of innocence on his face.

She yelps. The sound disappears with her body beneath the surface. Her husband wouldn't be too pleased with the antics; I know this. But my son Max is inside with their baby, trying to get the boy to take a nap.

He is teething.

Madonna Mia.

I know nothing about these things, and despite a lack of a role model, my boys are hands-on with their children.

My granddaughter Kelly, the only female born Butcher Girl, lies on a giant inflatable pelican. She is wearing pink sunglasses and a floppy sun hat that covers most of her tiny body. Nothing thaws this weathered old fool like my granddaughter does—she is my sunshine.

It's a good thing that I didn't have a daughter; I fear for my sanity and reason if I had.

"Mummy!" she screeches, excited. "Come up here with me. I'll keep you safe from the nutcase."

Bronson bursts into a fit of laughter that echoes the outdoor entertainment area. It's as wild as him. "Oh, don't you start, Outlaw."

Beside me, my eldest son Clay watches the gathering with the same contentment I thought neither of us would truly feel, yet undeniably do.

A sense of rest.

Comfort, even.

His wife is fast asleep on the sun lounger to his side with their twin boys, Luca—my namesake—and Ash, tucked under either arm. The boys are easily distinguished, Ash with his lighter hair and Luca with his thick frame.

A big boy.

Like me.

Clay's fingers are in her light-blonde hair, affectionately stroking the strands, and I somewhat miss having a woman find comfort in my touch.

My days of intimate love are done.

Now, I live each day for them. Making up for old times. It'll never be enough, but my grandchildren will know me and remember my commitment to them.

I will be present.

I will stay.

We have made lunch on Sundays a weekly tradition, though; I know who is to attribute these occasions. My sons aren't the leaders of this family anymore, nor I, my daughters-in-law reign. They pull us together.

Lucky men, really.

Too lucky.

Given the life we have lived.

As men, family time isn't naturally front and centre, but it is now. Especially since my youngest, Xander, has left the city. Left the legacy. To follow his own path. So, we come together for a weekly call with him from wherever he and his fiancé might be in the world.

China was the last destination.

I miss my boy.

But I had to let him go.

My other son, Konnor, lives hours from the District, but he makes the journey to see us during the school holidays.

When the sliding door runs along the tracks, I turn to watch Max stride outside with his son, Mattius, cradled in his arms and still clinging to consciousness.

"Should I try?" I ask before considering my lack of paternal skills. I rise to my feet, drawing Max's attention away from Cassidy who splashes Bronson by the poolside.

Dammit, I want to hold my grandson.

I feel damn useless at times.

My boys don't need me anymore, haven't for some time. Life doesn't tell you when the tables turn, and they grow larger than you and your teachings. Pride and melancholy both live in those moments of realisation.

He looks at me, a slight smirk hitting his lips. "Come with me. I'll show you how to get him to sleep."

Entirely too excited by the premise, like a damn old fool, I follow him across the lawn to the outdoor shower. It is a large rectangular space made from rustic wooden slats.

Max pulls his shirt off from the back of his collar and tosses the garment to the bench.

"Shirt off, old boy. He needs to feel your skin."

"That's enough of the old boy, *my boy*," I order.

"Just do it," Max says with that rare, settled smile, before stepping beneath the warm spray with the baby cradled in his tattooed arms. He rocks him as the water massages the child's stomach, and my chest swells with pride at how fatherhood looks on him.

The sun overhead forces Mattius to bat his eyes against the intrusion. It seems to have worked.

I was never the father my boys are, and I'm damn proud of them for being better than me. The weight of my failings sits heavily in my chest.

With that, I pull my shirt off and don't hesitate to step beneath the spray to join them.

Water droplets collect in Mattius' long lashes, and as he bats them out, his eyes eventually remain closed. Max carefully slides him into my arms; my grandson stays settled.

"You're stuck there now, *Nonnu*," Max announces pointedly, but I simply nod my agreement.

"That's fine." Mattius' tiny body is light and soft, a stark comparison to my muscular, hard frame. I look down at the vulnerable boy in my arms. In his face, I see versions of my boys, of myself. See the ghost of my late wife.

Were my sons this vulnerable once?

I suppose they were.

Max leaves me to join his wife in the pool, but not before shoving his brother Bronson into the water.

The splash brings laughter.

"Look at you," Bronson's wife, Shoshanna, says, ambling towards me with her son, Darius, carried in a sling and her other son, Stone, trudging after them. Evident in the grin and cake on his cheeks, Stone has been up to mischief. Of all my grandsons, I believe him to be the boldest. But I have four born within two months of each other, so we'll see what personalities arise. The chance to be more to them, to know them, sends a warm current through me.

I'll be better for them.

"*Nonnu*, I ate cake, Fawn, made, one," he yells with little consideration for the sleeping boy in my arms; such is a toddler's default volume, I have come to realise.

"*Shh*," I offer, low, to not scare Stone with my tone—he's a wildfire at times. Passionate. He reminds me of my youngest, Xander. "Mattius is sleeping, *se*? Did you start the cake without me, my boy?"

Shoshanna shakes her head. "He shoved his hands straight into the sponge cake Fawn baked for us. He ate one of the little fondant knight's heads off! I feel awful about it. Luckily, the dogs are inside licking the tiles clean." She bites her lower lip. "Do you think she'll be upset?"

"I wouldn't worry about Fawn." I keep my voice deep and quiet, rocking back and forth on instinct to lull my grandson. "It will take more than a ruined cake and some crumbs to bother that girl."

Shoshanna nods. "That's true." She eyes me for a moment. "Do you want my boys, too?"

Before I can answer, she pulls my grandson from her cloth-carrier and places him on the tiles, where he splashes in the puddles welling around my feet.

Then she tugs her denim shorts and shirt off, kicks her shoes to the grass, and joins her husband and the others in the shimmering blue water.

Stone plops down beside Darius, and now I'm minding three of my grandsons.

I look out over my family.

In the pool, Cassidy is wrapped around Max. She is the young ballerina girl who stopped us in our tracks and gave us hope for a life outside of the Family legacy—she gave us Kelly.

Young Fawn, drained from raising two Butcher brothers,

sleeps like an angel on the lounger—she is the last piece that connects us all.

And Shoshanna—I have known that girl for most of her life. She was my Bronson's childhood girlfriend. One he never let go of. I understand that kind of commitment to a woman. I have loved once and forever. Even went as far as to marry a woman I knew I could never fall in love with.

I didn't want to replace you, Maddie.

So, I married an unlovable woman.

My eyes coast across the backyard, taking in the sight of each of my sons with their partners. My chest squeezes in tight with sentiment so strong it's consuming.

Bronson: my wild boy. So much like my father. Max: my carbon copy. And Clay: more like our late Don, Jimmy, than me, in regrettable ways, but for his heart.

My boys.

My men.

My Butcher men.

from uncle xander

I LOVE MY
NEW
NEPHEWS!

CHINA

WISH YOU WERE
GLAMPING WITH US!

thank you

for your continued support, and for loving the Butcher *men* as much as I do.

Nicci Harris

XO

where it all started...

Max and Cassidy's story - book one and two.

Blurb:

The city's golden girl falls heart-first into a dark underworld.

I want two things in life: to be the leading ballerina in my academy—
And Max Butcher...

A massive, tattooed boxer, and renowned thug. And my very first
crush...

I may be a silly little girl to him, but he's intent on protecting,
possessing, and claiming me in every way—his little piece of purity.

But there is more to Max Butcher than the cold, cruel facade he
wears like armor. I know; I saw the broken boy inside him one day
when we were only children.

So, even as I stand in the shadows with him, as people get hurt...*as
people die...* I refuse to let him believe he's nothing more than a piece
in his family's corrupt empire.

There is good inside Max Butcher, and I refuse to let him live in the
dark forever.

nicci who?

I'm an Australian chick writing real love stories for dark
souls.
Stalk me.
**Meet other Butcher Boy lovers on Facebook. Join Harris's
Harem of Dark Romance Lovers
Stalk us.**

It's taken three years into my author career to write a
biography because, let's face it, you probably don't care that I
live in Australia, hate owls, am sober, or that my husband's
name is Ed—not Edward or Eddie—Ed... like who names
their son 'just' Ed? (love my in-laws, btw). Anyway, you

probably don't really care that my son's name is Jarrah—not Jarrod or Jason—to compensate for his dad's name *Ed*...

I ramble...

Here's what you really want to know. I'm a contradiction. Contradictory people are my jam. I am an independent woman who has lived her entire life doing things the wrong way, the impulsive way, the risky way... my way. I'm not from a rich family but I've taken wealthy people chances... I'm my own boss. I'm a full-time author, an Amazon best-seller, all despite the amount of people who said I couldn't, shouldn't, wouldn't... I'm that person.

So while I live a feminist kind of life... I write about men who kill, who control, who take their women like it's their last breath, pinning them down and whispering *"good girl"* and *"mine"* and *"you belong to me"* and all the red flag utterances that would have most independent women rolling their eyes so hard they see their brains.

I write about men who protect their women. Men who control them because they are so obsessed, so in love, they are terrified not to... Do I have daddy issues? *Probably.* Did I need to be controlled and protected more as a child and this is my outlet? *Possibly.*

So... if you don't like that... if you don't see the internal strength in my heroines, how they are the emotional rocks for these controlling *alphahole* men... then don't read my books. You won't like them. We can still be friends.

But I want both. I want my cake and to have a six-foot-five, tattooed, alphamale eat it too.

Made in the USA
Middletown, DE
07 November 2025

20904456R00073